Best Friend Insurance

Also by Beatrice Gormley

Fifth Grade Magic
Mail-Order Wings

J

Best Friend Insurance

by Beatrice Gormley

illustrated by Emily Arnold McCully

E. P. DUTTON   NEW YORK

Text copyright © 1983 by Beatrice Gormley
Illustrations copyright © 1983 by Emily Arnold McCully

All rights reserved. No part of this publication may be
reproduced or transmitted in any form or by any means,
electronic or mechanical, including photocopy, recording,
or any information storage and retrieval system now
known or to be invented, without permission in writing
from the publisher, except by a reviewer who wishes to
quote brief passages in connection with a review written
for inclusion in a magazine, newspaper, or broadcast.

Library of Congress Cataloging in Publication Data

Gormley, Beatrice.
    Best friend insurance.

    Summary: Just when Maureen feels she has been demoted
to second-best status by her former best friend Tracey,
a rather unusual insurance agent turns up, guaranteeing
replacement of lost friends within twenty-four hours.
    [1. Friendship—Fiction.   2. Cloning—Fiction]
I. McCully, Emily Arnold, ill.   II. Title.
PZ7.G6696Be   1983   [Fic]   83-5715
ISBN 0-525-44066-6

Published in the United States by E. P. Dutton, Inc.,
2 Park Avenue, New York, N.Y. 10016

Published simultaneously in Canada by Clarke,
Irwin & Company Limited, Toronto and Vancouver

Editor: Ann Durell   Designer: Isabel Warren-Lynch

Printed in the U.S.A.   W   First Edition

10 9 8 7 6 5 4 3 2 1

to my mother, Elizabeth F. LeCount

Contents

I Choose Maureen

Maureen Harrity stood on the playing field, basking in the June sunshine and waiting to be chosen for a kickball team. One of the captains was her best friend, Tracey Argos. So she just stood quietly at the edge of the jumping, yelling crowd, waiting to be picked.

In front of Tracey and the other captain, Amanda, one head with short, rough blonde hair stuck up above the others. That was Gwen, the tallest person in Miss Welgloss's class, even taller than Maureen. Gwen was tossing the kickball up and catching it again as she stared at Tracey, probably hoping Tracey would pick her right away because she was good at sports and because she and Tracey were on the swim team together. Maureen smiled to herself, pushing up the sleeves of her yellow blouse. Gwen should know better than that. That wasn't the way the kids' rules worked.

There was a method kids always followed in choosing teams, and everyone knew it just as well as if there were an official sign headed KIDS' RULES posted at the edge of the playing field. First you chose the best boy players. That made sure that you had a chance of winning the game. Next, you could afford to choose one girl—your best friend. Then you chose the boys who weren't such good players, and then you chose the rest of the girls.

As Tracey and Amanda started choosing boys, Maureen thought about how glad she was that she hadn't joined the swim team. She didn't like Gwen very much, and she would have had to see her at swim practice every morning as well as at school. Besides, Maureen wouldn't want to come to school with wet hair all the time, the way Tracey and Gwen did.

Now Tracey and Amanda each had three boys standing in back of them. It was Amanda's turn, and of course she would choose her best friend, Jody.

"I choose *Jody.*" Amanda gave a vigorous nod on the last word, making her long curls bob.

Jody took her place beside her friend, grinning. She must have felt the way Maureen was feeling—glad that today the ceremony of choosing teams was no problem for her. The protection of Tracey's friendship seemed to fit Maureen like a down vest, as warm as the sunshine on her back.

Tracey put her hand up to shade her eyes. Thinking that Tracey must be looking for her, Maureen moved out from the group so that Tracey could see her easily.

But Tracey's shiny brown eyes didn't meet Maureen's. Her gaze followed the kickball as it popped up from Gwen's hands and fell back down again.

"Well, come *on*, Tracey," said Amanda.

"Okay." Tracey's voice sounded carefully casual, and still she didn't look at Maureen. "I choose Gwen."

Maureen, who had started to step forward to join Tracey, stood frozen at the edge of the group. She felt the others staring at her, especially Jody and Amanda. She saw Gwen saunter up to Tracey and turn, smiling right at Maureen, as she flipped the kickball from one hand to another. There they stood, plump Tracey and tall, lean Gwen. Together.

The sun was still shining on Maureen's back, but she didn't feel warm anymore. She felt the way she felt in one of her worst dreams, when she went to school just as if everything were normal—and then realized in the classroom that she had forgotten to put on her clothes. If only she would wake up!

Maureen saw Jody lean toward Amanda to whisper, and saw her lips move: "Choose Maureen." That was like Jody, who hated to see anyone's feelings hurt. But Maureen wished she would just pretend not to notice what Tracey had done to her.

Anyway, Amanda didn't seem to hear, or maybe she

thought she ought to stick to the unwritten rules about choosing teams. "I choose Marvin."

Marvin Smith was a logical next choice, too small and skinny to be a strong kicker, but quick. "Super-Smith!" he called out, leaping toward Amanda's group with a gesture like Superman flying.

Now Tracey, with Gwen leaning down to whisper advice, chose another boy. As the rest of the boys joined one team or the other, Maureen wondered if she should just walk off the field. She didn't *have* to stand here like a jerk. What if Tracey didn't choose her at all? She wasn't such a great kickball player, and she might actually be the last person chosen! That hadn't happened to her for a long time, but it might happen today.

"I choose Maureen." Tracey's voice was matter-of-fact, her dark eyes blank. She turned toward Amanda, as if she were only thinking of hearing the other captain's next choice. As if she hadn't announced, just as plainly as huge letters from a skywriting airplane, "I choose Gwen for my new best friend. I choose Maureen for my old second-best friend."

Maureen could still walk off the field, turning her back on treacherous Tracey. But if she left, she would get a reputation as a poor sport. And the next time sides were chosen, Maureen really would be chosen last.

All right. Maureen would act like a good sport and play on Tracey's team in this game. But one thing was sure—she would *not* be Tracey Argos's second-best friend. She would not even speak to Tracey, unless Tracey came to her and begged her to be best friends again.

The team choosing was finished. Amanda's team, up first, gathered around home plate. The boys and girls on Tracey's team crowded around her, shouting, "Pitcher!" "Catcher!" "First base!" But Maureen walked away, muttering to no one in particular, "I'm left field." No one else would want that position, and it would put her and her feelings as far away from the other kids as possible.

By the time recess was over, Maureen was still going over and over the same miserable thoughts, as if she were trying to erase something written in ink and just wearing a hole in the paper. Slumping into her seat in the classroom, Maureen felt sick of thinking about Tracey, but she couldn't help it. The thought she kept coming back to was, How could Tracey treat me like that? She would never, ever, have done that to Tracey, or to any other best friend. The fair thing to do, if you started to like another friend better, would be to let the first friend know gradually—and certainly not in public, in front of the whole class.

Miss Welgloss, the teacher, blew her nose. "Let's settle down quickly, everybody, please. Gwen? Marvin? Thank you. I don't want to waste any time, because we're lucky to have a visitor, Mr.—"

"—Santa Claus," whispered Marvin from his seat behind Jody. In spite of her misery, Maureen smiled a little, because the man standing at the front of the room with Miss Welgloss did look sort of like a middle-aged Santa. It wasn't just his silvery mustache and hair, or the pinkness of his round face, or the generous way he filled out his red slacks and striped jacket—it was also the feeling of good cheer that seemed to beam from him as he looked around the room.

"—Mr. Costue, of Costue and Fader Insurance Company," Miss Welgloss was saying. "Mr. Costue was kind enough to take the time to come in and talk to us about insurance. As I told you, Mr. Costue, this is so helpful for us, because we're going to be doing projects on careers, and we want to find out about as many different careers as possible." She stepped to the chalkboard, wrote *Insurance Agent*, and wiped her nose again. "Excuse me," she said to Mr. Costue. "I get such awful hay fever this time of year. I'll go sit in the back, and you can take right over."

Mr. Costue smiled around the room again, as if he was glad to be with all of them. For a second his eyes met Maureen's, seeming to notice her especially, and her spirits lifted. It was impossible to feel miserable when such a comfortable, friendly-looking man was smiling right at her. Then his glance moved on. "What is insurance?" His voice was rich and mellow. "What can an insurance agent do for people, exactly? The answer is—security. Insurance gives security. An insurance agent's job is to make people more secure. Take life insurance, for instance. . . ."

Maureen let Mr. Costue's soothing voice fade into the background. Everything and everyone in the classroom seemed shadowy to her, except herself and the sort of raw feeling all over her skin, and Tracey and Gwen sitting in the next row. The only thing that could make Maureen feel better would be Tracy coming to her and saying, "I didn't really mean it. I just chose Gwen because I felt sorry for her . . . because I owed her fifty cents . . . because my mother told me to. . . ."

Mr. Costue was pulling down the screen in front of the chalkboard. "I think these charts will help make the idea of insurance a little clearer," he said. He switched on the overhead projector in the middle of the room. "Could someone get the lights and shades? . . . Fine. Now, for example, this chart . . ."

Maureen felt better in the darkened classroom. She couldn't see Tracey and Gwen very well, and no one, like Jody or Amanda, could give her pitying glances. Without really seeing, she watched Mr. Costue's charts and graphs come and go on the screen. Without really hearing, she listened to the pleasant drone of his words.

And then her eyes popped open, and she sat up straight. She was seeing things! It looked as if the chart now on the screen was titled Rate of Best Friend Loss.

She must be so upset about Tracey that she couldn't see straight. Maureen twisted around to stare at Mr. Costue.

". . . shows the average rate of loss of best friends among fifth-grade girls," he was saying calmly.

Maureen whipped back to face the screen. The title was still the same. What was going on?

Maureen turned to her left, then to her right, peering through the half dark. Didn't anyone else see what she saw, hear what she heard? The other kids seemed to have lost all interest in insurance, if they ever had any.

But turning to look at Mr. Costue again, Maureen noticed Marvin, sitting behind Jody and right next to the projector. He was staring at the screen, his mouth open a little. Maureen wasn't the *only* one who was paying attention.

Mr. Costue's voice flowed on, as if he were still talking about life insurance. "You notice the average fifth-grade girl will lose her best friend within six months." He put a finger on the midpoint of the line climbing upwards across the chart. "Well, but maybe you think you're special. Maybe you're sure you're the lucky one in two hundred girls who's going to keep her best friend for a year or more. Hm?"

Maureen's cheeks burned.

"And maybe you will be lucky," said Mr. Costue. "I hope all of you will be. But let me leave you with this

8

thought: *Only* friend insurance can guarantee another best friend if you lose the one you have." The insurance man paused impressively. Then, in a brisk tone, he said, "Lights?"

As the lights went on, Gwen's snicker rose above the classroom murmuring. "Look at Miss Welgloss!"

Everyone turned to stare at the teacher, blinking and yawning in her chair at the back of the room. "I must have nodded off for a second," she said with an embarrassed laugh. "It's these pills I have to take for my allergies."

Mr. Costue laughed too in a friendly way, waving his hand. "I've been known to put people to sleep before! Well, thank you so much for—"

"Thank *you*, Mr. Costue!" Miss Welgloss stood up, starting to clap. "We all appreciate your visit so much, and we learned so much about insurance, didn't we?" The class followed her lead in clapping, although Maureen heard two whispers under the applause: "Boring" from Gwen, and "Weird, really weird" from Marvin.

"Now," said Miss Welgloss, "who would like to show Mr. Costue the way back to the office? Amanda, why don't—"

"How about this girl in the yellow blouse?" asked Mr. Costue. "What's your name?"

He was looking right at Maureen.

You're the one I want to talk to, his twinkling blue eyes seemed to tell her. Out of all these people, you're the one. Her heart thumped. She felt sure that if anyone could help her, it would be Mr. Costue. "Maureen," she gasped.

"Fine. Maureen, you escort our guest, then." Miss Welgloss still looked groggy, as if she could have slept another hour or so. "And thank you again, Mr. Costue."

Friend Insurance?

Leading Mr. Costue down the hall toward the office, Maureen looked at him sideways. Now that she had a chance to talk to him alone, she felt shy. In the classroom she had such a strong feeling that he wanted to say something to her in particular—but maybe she had been wrong.

The insurance man smiled down at her, the corners of his pale blue eyes creasing. "I have a feeling that you want to ask me a question, Maureen."

This was her chance—her chance to ask him about that last chart. But maybe she had somehow misunderstood. Maybe it had been just for fun, a humorous example. Mr. Costue seemed like the kind of person who might joke around.

What if it wasn't a joke, though? What if Mr. Costue *really sold friend insurance,* and Maureen missed this chance?

"Er, Mr. Costue, that last chart you showed—that was just a joke, wasn't it?" Maureen blushed as she said it. Now he would laugh at her.

But the insurance man's broad pink face was serious. "No, not at all. I don't think losing friends is funny—do you?"

Maureen stared back at him. "No. . . . But—but, *friend* insurance—there couldn't really be any such thing." They were outside the office now. She had to find out. She stopped and turned to face him, clasping her hands together.

Mr. Costue stopped, too. For a moment he just gazed down at her, as if he was sizing her up. Then he shifted his briefcase to the other hand, pushing his free hand into the pocket of his red pants. "Yes," he said quietly. "I wouldn't tell this to everyone—it's not something that should get around to teachers or parents. But yes, I do carry friend insurance. And I have a certain feeling, Maureen, that friend insurance is just what you need."

Maureen blushed again, embarrassed that a stranger could guess she had friend trouble. On the other hand, Mr. Costue was so understanding and friendly, he hardly seemed like a stranger. "I don't know," she said. "I don't understand how it could work."

"Very simply." Mr. Costue leaned toward her confidentially, the ends of his silver mustache wiggling as he talked. "It's hard to believe that no other insurance company has come up with friend insurance, in this age of molecular biology and compu—" A look of dismay flicked over Mr. Costue's pink face, but was instantly lost in his hearty laugh. "Not that molecular biology has anything to do with insurance! I just meant that friend insurance is a thoroughly up-to-date, forward-looking idea. The way it works is, someone—yourself, for instance—buys a friend insurance policy from us. Then, if you lose your friend, we replace her with another best friend—within twenty-four hours."

"But—" Maureen still didn't see how they could replace a friend, even though Mr. Costue had just explained it to her. It didn't matter for *her*, though, she realized with a pang. "Anyway, it's too late for me. I already lost my friend."

"Why, that's too bad, Maureen." Mr. Costue's tone was gentle, but his eyes seemed to sparkle. "I'm sorry to hear that. But it's *not* too late! You see, as a special introductory offer to celebrate the opening of the Costue and Fader office in Rushfield, we are selling *retroactive* policies. That means, Maureen, that if you buy a policy now, we will replace one *previously* lost friend, without any surcharge. So how about it, Maureen? Fifty dollars for the first six months' premium."

"Fifty dollars!" Maureen's spirits, which had been

cautiously rising, fell down with a bump. "Fifty dollars!" Angry with Mr. Costue for getting her hopes up, she turned away. "You must think my father's a millionaire."

"It *is* a lot of money," agreed Mr. Costue sympathetically, "but business is business. You don't get something for nothing." He paused, then snapped his fingers as if an idea had struck him. "Say, Maureen! I think maybe we can make a deal."

Afraid to hope, Maureen turned back. "What do you mean?"

Mr. Costue's smile seemed to warm her face. "I mean, I could use your help, Maureen! It would easily be worth fifty dollars. I have a job that only you could do for me. It won't take much time, but it's *very* important." Setting his briefcase down, he bent over and pulled out two papers. "What do you think? Could you come to my office this afternoon? It's right near the A&P. Is that too far from your house?"

"No," said Maureen quickly. "I could ride my bike. But what kind of—"

"I mustn't keep you out of class any longer," interrupted Mr. Costue, "so I'll explain everything at the office. This is for you, Maureen—your policy, and your Friend Loss Report." He handed the papers to her. "Just fill out the report at home, and bring it to my office as soon as you can. And then, within twenty-four hours—" He spread his hands.

"A new friend?" whispered Maureen.

Mr. Costue nodded, beaming at her as if they had a special understanding. He pulled open the door of the office. "See you later, Maureen."

Walking back down the hall, Maureen examined the papers in her hand. The white paper on top was headed Friend Insurance Policy under an insignia like two ribbons twisted around each other. The policy seemed to be full of phrases like "hereinafter called the Insured" and "in case of fraudulent or material misrepresentation." Maureen decided to read it later.

The second paper was pink, also topped by the twisted ribbons insignia. Friend Loss Report, it said.

It was so strange. Friend insurance! A minute ago, talking to Mr. Costue, Maureen had felt that friend insurance was entirely possible. But now, looking at these papers, she wondered if it was some kind of hoax.

If you lost a friend, no one could replace her for you. You had to get her back or make a new friend—or get along without one. Maureen felt her face turn red. Had Mr. Costue picked her out because she looked gullible?

But then she remembered Mr. Costue's sympathetic expression when she told him she had lost her friend. She remembered the warmth he gave off like the June sun, and her feeling that she could count on him. She couldn't believe he would play a cruel joke on her.

It was just that nobody had ever heard of friend insurance before. A lot of things, like television, would seem impossible if you weren't used to the idea. But if you were used to television, it didn't seem impossible at all, even though you didn't know how it worked.

Satisfied, Maureen folded the papers up small and stuffed them into her skirt pocket. Mr. Costue *would* come up with a new friend for her, maybe one much better than Tracey. Without looking at Tracey, Maureen swung through the classroom door and walked to her seat with a bouncy step to show Tracey she didn't care. That would start her wondering. And then when Maureen appeared with a new friend—!

Sliding into her seat, Maureen realized that an argument was going on between Miss Welgloss and Marvin. "How about tomorrow afternoon instead?" the teacher was saying. "Since we've already had one talk this afternoon."

"But you told me to be ready today!" Marvin was half out of his seat with one knee on his chair, his slight frame stiff with indignation. "That's why I brought my model to school. Anyway, Tuesday afternoons are supposed to be for science, and that Santa Claus insurance guy didn't have anything to do with science. That really wasn't fair." He gave the teacher a reproachful stare.

Miss Welgloss shook her head, smiling a little as if Marvin was too much for her. "Yes, but this happened to be the only day Mr. Costue could come in, and we're running short of time for our career projects."

"Frankly, Miss Welgloss," said Marvin, "I think I can help a lot more with careers than he did. Nobody wants to grow up to be an insurance man. And when I was making my model, I found out what it's like to be a molecular biologist, which is a really good career. Anyway, if you ask me, I think there was something very weird about—"

"Oh, all right, Marvin, go ahead, only don't—ah-*choo!*—take too long." Wiping her nose, the teacher sat down at the side of the room. "So you made this model at a special science course you took during spring vacation?"

"Yep." Marvin swung a paper bag from one hand as he scampered to the front of the room. "It was a course in molecular biology, which is the wave of the future, in case anyone doesn't know. And my model is a DNA molecule, the key to the secret of life itself!" Dramatically he pulled from the bag a long object like a twisted rope ladder, with flat plastic cable for the sides and strings of colored beads for the rungs.

"Isn't Marvin a bright little monkey," said Gwen. "He can string beads."

There was some laughter and murmuring. Marvin actually did look something like a monkey, in a likeable way, thought Maureen. But it was mean of Gwen to say that.

The noise died away as Miss Welgloss looked around, frowning. "Let's be courteous to Marvin, since he's doing us the favor of sharing his project."

Marvin shot a look of cold hatred at Gwen. Then he turned back to his model, dangling it from one hand.

"Okay. Here's the amazing thing: This molecule is really smaller than the point of a pin, but it has all the information you need to make a whole person!"

"That is amazing," said the teacher. "And where is this molecule in the body?"

"It's in every single cell!" Marvin twisted his model so that the beads flashed as the rungs revolved. "That's why it's so easy to clone people. All you need is one little skin cell, or any cell—hair, fingernails, whatever—and you could make a whole person, just like the first one! For instance, the army could clone some really strong guy, and take over the world."

"Wait a minute, wait a minute." Miss Welgloss held up her hands, laughing. "I think you're getting into science fiction, Marvin. I think scientists are a long way from growing clones of people."

Marvin shook his head, running his free hand along the twists of one cable. "Miss Welgloss, all the information they need is right here in the DNA, the genes."

"But it's very, very complicated information, isn't it?"

"Yeah," said Marvin eagerly, "but that's where computers come in. A computer can take in all these tiny little details"—he flicked a bead with his finger—"and sort it out for the molecular biologists who grow the clones."

The teacher smiled to herself, but she didn't contradict him, and Marvin went on to explain how the chemicals in the molecule fit together. As he talked, Maureen wondered who was right, Marvin or Miss Welgloss? Marvin did know a lot about science, but he also read a lot of science fiction, and maybe he got them mixed up.

"Thank you, Marvin," said the teacher as he slid his model back into the bag. "Now I'm going to see if I can clone myself, so that *I* can stay home tomorrow and nurse my hay fever."

The class laughed. "Don't anybody clone Marvin," whispered Gwen loudly. "One kid who looks like Curious George is enough."

Marvin gave Gwen another look, as if he thought one of her was more than enough. Maureen agreed with him. Why did Tracey have to pick a mean person like Gwen for a friend, instead of someone they could both like?

"All right, I didn't mean to make fun of your project, Marvin. That's an outstanding model, and I'm giving you an extra-credit check plus for your talk." Moving back to her desk, Miss Welgloss picked up her grade book. "Now, before the bell rings, let me remind you all about our field trip to the Blue Hills Reservation on Friday. Amanda, would you pass out these permission slips? It's supposed to be nice weather at the end of the week, and after the nature walk we're going to hike up to the observation tower."

Amanda, handing Maureen a permission slip,

paused. "Are we supposed to choose partners for this trip?"

"Oh, yes," the teacher answered. "I guess we should pair off for the hike."

Seeing Amanda exchange a look of understanding with Jody, Maureen turned without thinking toward Tracey. But Tracey was twisted around in her seat, whispering with Gwen. "Okay," Maureen heard Tracey say.

Okay! Maureen jerked her eyes away from Tracey and sat up straight, lifting her chin. She didn't have a partner yet, but she would have one within twenty-four hours. Mr. Costue had promised.

As Amanda moved on, Jody leaned across the aisle to Maureen, her gaze kind under her straight bangs. "You could go with us," she whispered.

Maureen flushed at Jody's sympathy. "No, thanks," she said politely. All she wanted to do now was to go home and fill out the form and take it to Mr. Costue's office, so that he could get to work on replacing her best friend.

As Maureen trotted along Main Street away from the school, swinging her book bag, she felt the Friend Loss Report and the insurance policy crackle inside her pocket. "All right, Tracey," she said to herself, "go ahead and be friends with Gwen. I couldn't care less!" *I couldn't care less*—that had a nice ring to it.

But—Maureen slowed down, stepping over the

cracks in the sidewalk and frowning. How *was* Mr. Costue going to replace her best friend? Would he pick someone else in Maureen's class, someone like Jody? Or would he bring her someone she didn't even know now, some girl who was just the right person to be Maureen's friend?

Lifting her gaze from the sidewalk, Maureen noticed two younger girls walking about a block ahead of her. One of them was a familiar figure in a green jumper, her wispy light brown hair floating up and down as she skipped and chattered—Maureen's little sister, Alison. Maureen didn't recognize the other girl, who wore glasses. Alison was always bringing home someone different. Alison didn't seem to care about having one close friend, the way Maureen did.

Maureen followed Alison and the other girl up the winding slopes of Chestnut Hill Road, under the horse chestnut trees with their fat clusters of white blossoms. When she got home Maureen would check in with her mother and tell her she was going to ride her bike to the dime store. Then she would go to her room and fill out the report form Mr. Costue had given her, and then she would ride to his office near the A&P. On the way home she would stop at the dime store and get some stickers or a candy bar or something, so that she wouldn't have lied to her mother.

Here was the Harritys' blue gray shingled house, built into the hill with the garage underneath. As she turned in the driveway, Maureen saw Alison and her friend hopping up the garden steps from the driveway to the back door. They would go into the family room and play one of Alison's many board games.

Mom was probably studying in her basement office. Pulling up one of the garage doors, Maureen edged between the station wagon and the bicycles next to the garage wall. As she opened the door at the back of the garage, she saw light shining from the half-open office door into the dim basement. "Mom?"

Report Loss Promptly

As Maureen poked her head in the door, Mrs. Harrity was leaning forward with her elbows on the desk, taking notes from a book. She finished writing something in her notebook and stretched, smiling vaguely at her daughter. "Hi, Maureen. How was your day? Did Alison come home?"

"Uh-huh." Maureen squeezed into the office and sat down on the dehumidifier. "She's upstairs. She brought home one of her weird little friends."

Giving Maureen a reproving look, Mrs. Harrity smoothed her already smooth light brown hair from her forehead to the clasp at the back of her head. "Alison's friends aren't weird." Then she gazed at Maureen, her deep-set eyes more thoughtful. "I bet they'd like to have you join in their Sorry game, or whatever they're playing."

"I bet they wouldn't," said Maureen. "Anyway, I hate Sorry. It's a stupid baby game."

"All right," said her mother. She picked up her textbook.

"Mom . . ." Maureen had thought she had gotten over being upset about Tracey, but now that she was with her mother, the memory of that awful naked feeling came rushing back.

Her mother looked up again, raising her eyebrows.

"Tracey was acting funny today."

"Oh, that's what's bothering you." Leaning back, Mrs. Harrity took a sip from her coffee mug. "What do you mean, funny?"

"Well—" Maureen started to tell her mother about choosing kickball teams, but it seemed too complicated to explain about kids' rules and all that stuff. But the field trip was different. "She's going to be partners with Gwen instead of me on the field trip."

Her mother shrugged. "Probably Tracey just wants to spend some time with someone else, for a change. And *I* think you've gotten in the habit of counting too much on Tracey. Why don't you ask someone else to be your partner?"

Standing up, Maureen pushed her hands into her pockets. Mr. Costue was right—there would be no point in telling parents about friend insurance. When you lost a friend, they were full of helpful advice that was no help at all. "You don't understand, Mom. Never mind." She backed out the door. "Anyway, I'm going to ride my bike to the dime store, okay?" Without waiting for an answer, she ran up the stairs from the basement to the kitchen, her book bag bumping against each step.

Pausing in the kitchen to grab a handful of raisins from the cupboard, Maureen saw Alison and the girl with glasses sitting on the carpet in the family room, hunched over the Sorry board. Alison gave her an unfriendly glance. "You can't play with us."

"Don't want to," said Maureen, munching raisins. She knew Alison was trying to get back at Maureen for not letting her play last Saturday when Tracey had come over. But Maureen had something better to do this afternoon than play Sorry!

"Well, good riddance to bad rubbish!" called Alison.

Jogging down the hall to her bedroom, Maureen laughed to herself. Good riddance to bad rubbish. Alison thought that was a really snappy insult.

Just as Maureen reached her room, she heard the phone ring in the kitchen. "Maureen!" Alison bawled down the hall. "Telephone!"

Maureen trotted back to the kitchen. "Who is it?"

In the family room and at her Sorry game again,

Alison shrugged her small shoulders. "How would I know?"

"You could have asked." Maureen picked up the phone. "Hello?"

"Hi." It was Tracey. "Hey, you aren't mad at me, are you?" She laughed, as though it was silly of her to wonder.

Maureen felt blood surge into her face. This was her chance to tell Tracey off. "I couldn't care less," she would say.

No, this was her chance to make up with Tracey, to get her best friend back. That was what she really wanted. "I don't know, after the way you were acting today," she said coolly.

"Maureen, don't be so touchy." Tracey sighed. "In the first place, I didn't think you cared that much about kickball. You were just sort of standing there, looking bored. Then, after I chose Gwen before you, I realized you were upset, but you shouldn't have been. It wasn't anything against you. It's just that Gwen's a better athlete, and I wanted to have a good team."

"And what about partners for the field trip?" asked Maureen sarcastically. "I suppose you wanted to go with Gwen because she's so good at hiking?"

"Maureen, it's hard to explain things to you if you're going to be like that." Tracey's tone was reproachful. "It's just that Gwen asked me first, that's all. If you had asked me first, I would have been your partner. So why should you be mad at me?"

Maureen struggled with herself. If Tracey really meant it, why should Maureen hold a grudge against her? It sounded as if Tracey was sorry, and still wanted to be best friends. "All right," said Maureen finally. "Never mind. Do you want to come over this Saturday?"

"Oh, I really wish I could," said Tracey, "but I have to go to a swim meet Saturday. Some other time, okay? Well, I'm glad you aren't mad at me. See you tomorrow."

Gripping the receiver so hard that her arm ached, Maureen listened to the buzzing of the phone. So Tracey thought she could have things exactly the way she wanted. She wanted to have Gwen for a best friend, to be partners with and play sports with, and she wanted Maureen to wait around for her as a second-best friend, a backup friend.

Slowly putting down the phone, Maureen turned toward the family room. Alison and her friend were bent over the Sorry board, laughing. They probably weren't laughing at her—but she felt furious, just the same. "Aren't you two a little old for that baby game?" she called.

"Mommy!" yelled Alison immediately. "Maureen's bothering us!"

Maureen felt like rushing into the family room and kicking their stupid Sorry board all the way across the carpet. Instead she made a face at Alison and stalked down the hall to her bedroom.

Pulling the Friend Loss Report and the Friend Insurance Policy from her pocket, she sat down at her desk. "Report loss promptly!" it said at the top of the pink paper.

All right. That was just what Maureen would do. She took a pencil from the desk drawer and began to fill out the report. There were spaces for her name, address, phone number. Name of lost friend. Brief description of lost friend. *Shiny brown eyes,* wrote Maureen. *Good at talking people into things.*

The next section, Circumstances of Loss, Maureen filled out hastily. If she thought too much about it, she would get upset all over again. She went right on to Family Environment: "To make sure that your new friend will be compatible with your family as well as yourself, please complete fully and carefully." There was a blank for her mother's name and age. *Kathleen MacQueen Harrity,* wrote Maureen. *Age 38.* Then her father: *Frank J. Harrity. Age 39.*

Next to the blank for each name was a peel-off strip with the direction, "IMPORTANT: Peel off and stick a hair or fingernail clipping from this parent here."

Hair or nail clipping?

This sounded so strange that Maureen read it over again, frowning. Why in the world would the insurance company want her mother's and father's hairs and nail clippings? That seemed creepy—like voodoo, or something. Maybe she could just skip that part.

But the report continued: "DO NOT OMIT! Necessary to evaluate biological compatibility."

That was different, then. Of course Mr. Costue, a regular businessman, wouldn't have anything to do with voodoo. Maureen laughed uneasily. This was just the complicated scientific way to fill out a loss report form. Hadn't Mr. Costue said something about the "advances in molecular biology"? But no, he had said that *didn't* have anything to do with insurance.

Anyway, Maureen had better go ahead and fill in the report the way it said to. If she didn't, the insurance company might just send it back to her, the way Miss Welgloss sometimes did worksheets, with a red-pencilled *Incomplete* across the top.

In her parents' bedroom at the end of the hall, Maureen searched the tops of their dressers. She pulled a light brown hair from her mother's brush. On her father's dresser there was nothing but matchbooks and business cards, but in his closet, on the shoulder of a dark jacket, she found one of his short gray hairs.

Back at her desk, Maureen coiled her mother's hair around her little finger and stuck it onto the proper sticky strip. Her father's hair was so short that she just stuck it on straight. There. On to the next section.

Your New Best Friend.   What is the most important characteristic that you would like your new best friend to have?

A few blank lines followed. Without hesitating, Maureen wrote, *She should always like me, no matter what.*

Finished. Standing up, Maureen slipped the Friend Insurance Policy into the desk drawer, out of sight, and folded the report to put back in her pocket.

A short while later, Maureen braked her bicycle in front of the A&P. Last week, when she was here doing errands with her mother, that office beside the A&P had been empty, with a For Rent sign in the window. Now the window was stencilled with black and gold letters: Costue and Fader Insurance Co. On the other side of the window Mr. Costue was sitting at a desk with his coat off, his silvery head bent over some papers.

As Maureen opened the door, Mr. Costue jumped up, his ruddy face beaming. "Well, Maureen! You found the office all right, hm? And what about the report? You didn't have any trouble filling that out, did you? I mean filling it out *completely.*"

"Here it is." Maureen unfolded the pink report form, handling it carefully so that the hairs wouldn't fall off, and held it out to Mr. Costue. "I hope I did it right. But Mr. Costue, I didn't understand . . ."

"Ah." Mr. Costue's silver mustache twitched as he stared at Maureen's report. "Well done, Maureen. You carried out the instructions so well. Good for you." He slipped the report into a manila envelope stamped Top

Priority. "Now, Maureen, let me get you started on that very important work that you promised to do for me."

But Maureen wasn't really listening, because she had noticed the plants in the middle of the room. What a lot of plants—potted palms in front of the room divider, ferns sprouting out of the top, spider plants cascading down from pots hung above the ferns. It was like a little jungle blocking off the back of the office. But Maureen could see through the fern fronds the hood of a computer terminal, and she heard an electronic beeping.

Maureen became aware that Mr. Costue was looking at her, waiting for her response. "Oh—I'm sorry, Mr. Costue. The work? I can stay until about five thirty, and then I have to go home for dinner." Rising on tiptoes, she saw that the computer terminal was set into the far side of a row of metal cabinets.

"I'll need your full attention about this," said Mr. Costue in a serious voice. Immediately Maureen turned back to him, and he went on, "Because this is important work. But it's not office work. It's field work, a very sensitive assignment." Opening a file drawer, he took out a sheaf of leaflets. "And I think you're just the person for the job, Maureen. Perceptive, observant—hm?" He smiled and winked, as if of course he wouldn't expect her to agree to those compliments, but just the same they were true.

Feeling a pleasant glow, Maureen held out her hand for the leaflets. They had the same twisted ribbons sign on the front that she had noticed on her policy and her report form.

Mr. Costue tapped a forefinger on the twisted ribbons. "That, Maureen, is the friend insurance symbol. Two lives entwined in friendship. And the purpose of these leaflets is to explain to other girls about friend insurance. You see, Maureen, the other girls in your class—like most other girls, I would say—didn't catch on as easily as you did. They need friend insurance, but they also need to have it explained to them."

"Do you really think *they* need it?" Maureen wondered if Mr. Costue understood kids as well as she had assumed. "I haven't noticed that."

Mr. Costue gazed at her patiently. "Everyone needs friend insurance, Maureen. Your one defect, if you don't mind my saying so—it's really a nice kind of defect—is that you underestimate yourself. *Everyone* needs friend insurance! But most people just don't realize it." He plucked one of the leaflets from Maureen's hand. "Here, let me show you. Each leaflet points out a potential friend loss situation."

He opened the leaflet to show a cartoon of a girl in gym clothes, holding a kickball, with a stuck-up look on her face. In the background a few other girls were looking at her and whispering behind their hands. The caption read, "Think everyone admires you because you're good at sports? Think again!" Then a few paragraphs on the next page went on to explain about friend insurance, with a little chart like the one Mr. Costue had showed in the classroom.

"Now, tell me, Maureen," said Mr. Costue, "is there a girl in your class who should get this leaflet?"

"I think so," said Maureen. "That's like Gwen. But I never—"

"I knew you'd take to this like a duck to water, Maureen!" The insurance salesman beamed at her. "And it's so important to match the right message to the right person, because each leaflet is different, you see."

Maureen shook her head wonderingly. "I never thought of Gwen that way before."

"Probably she didn't either." Mr. Costue nodded earnestly. "You see, Maureen, that's the purpose of these leaflets—to wake up each girl to the potential dangers of her particular situation." He handed the leaflet back to her. "Well, I can see my judgment was right—you're the perfect person for this job! I want you to distribute one leaflet (the right one, of course, and I leave that up to you) to each girl in your class. Can you do that tomorrow?"

Maureen thought a moment. "I could go to school early and put them on the desks before anyone else gets there."

"That's using your head, Maureen. Of course you understand this isn't something that teachers or parents need to know about."

Maureen did understand. Out of all the kids in her class, she *was* the right person to help Mr. Costue, she thought proudly. "Should I pass out insurance policies and Friend Loss Report forms, too?"

But Mr. Costue felt that would be too much at once. "They aren't as quick on the uptake as you are, Maureen." He asked Maureen for the other girls' addresses, so he could send a policy and report form to each one in the mail "along with a note that they can turn in the report *before* loss, to speed things up."

Maureen was pleased that she could tell him where most of the girls in her class lived. Not the house numbers, of course, but Mr. Costue could get them from the telephone book.

"Excellent, Maureen, excellent!" Writing down the last address, Mr. Costue stood up.

Just then the beeping from the machine behind the divider stopped. A man's voice announced, "The data bank is all set to accept that genetic data, Will, if you want to pass it over to me."

Mr. Costue stiffened, the satisfied expression fading from his face. "Not now," he said without turning around.

Maureen craned her neck, trying to peer through the tangle of plants around the room divider. She caught a glimpse of a droopy face and lank dark hair above the computer terminal hood.

"But Will," the other man began, "you said you wanted—"

"*Not now,*" barked Mr. Costue. Maureen hadn't heard him use that tone before. She tried to get another glimpse, but he grasped her by the elbow and steered her out the door. "Again," he said in his usual friendly tone, "thanks so much, Maureen. I'm counting on you!" Laughingly he jerked his head back toward the office. "If I had to depend on Fader for everything, I'd be in a pickle!"

Maureen laughed too, although she didn't understand why Mr. Costue was angry with the other man —his partner, Mr. Fader, she supposed. But Mr. Fader *had* looked sort of spacy. She started toward her bike, then turned back, remembering. "What about my—my"—she glanced around quickly, and whispered the last words—"my friend?"

Mr. Costue stuck his pink face out the office door, winking at her confidentially. "Within twenty-four hours, Maureen. Trust me!"

Within Twenty-four Hours

It didn't take Maureen long that evening to find the right leaflet for each person. This one, for instance, was perfect for Tracey.

The picture showed two girls, one plump and the other tall and lean, walking together. The plump girl was smiling as if nothing was wrong, but the tall girl was looking sideways at the plump girl's waist. The caption read, "Is plump really pleasing? Does your friend like to be seen with a fatty?"

Maureen hummed a little tune as she sorted through the leaflets, looking for something for Amanda.

Opening the classroom door a crack next morning, Maureen was relieved that no one else was there yet. She scooted in and moved swiftly among the desks. She had been smart to decide beforehand who should get which leaflet. Not all of them had been as easy to pick out as Tracey and Gwen.

But amazingly enough, there really was a leaflet that seemed to match each girl. Maureen wouldn't have believed it, but every single girl in her classroom had something to be afraid of—a particular way in which she could lose friends.

No time to think about it now. Did she put a leaflet on each girl's desk? Yes. Now to get out of here, before anyone else came.

Zipping out of the room, Maureen tried to stride along confidently, as if she had nothing to hide. But that was silly, because she had come to school so early that there was no one else in the hall. She had time to go out the back way and come in with the other kids, as if she had just arrived.

A short while later, as Miss Welgloss blew her nose and took attendance, Maureen cast careful glances around to see if the other girls were reading their leaflets. Tracey's leaflet seemed to be getting to her, all right. Her plump face was red, and she had turned around to show it to Gwen, whispering indignantly.

But Gwen raised her eyebrows and smiled. "Well, you aren't exactly skinny," she said, loudly enough for Maureen and several others to hear.

"So what did yours say, if you're so perfect?" demanded Tracey. But Gwen just scowled, crumpling her leaflet into a ball and shoving it into her desk.

It was gratifying, the way the leaflets were affecting Tracey and Gwen. But turning to her left, Maureen felt a qualm at the expression she saw on Jody's face. Maybe Maureen shouldn't have given her that leaflet. "Nicey-nice isn't always nice—sometimes it's just boring," it had said.

Maureen herself didn't think Jody was boring, but she had heard other girls make remarks like that about Jody. Even Amanda had said once, "Nobody could really be *that* nice!"

Amanda didn't look very happy right now, either. She was staring down at her leaflet, holding on to her curly locks with both hands. Amanda's leaflet had hinted at diseases that made the hair fall out, Maureen remembered. It had suggested that some girls were popular only because they were pretty—at the moment. Was Amanda's lower lip trembling? Stirring uneasily, Maureen looked away.

"Hey, what are those?" whispered Marvin, leaning over Jody's shoulder. "I didn't get one. Where'd they come from? What's it say?"

"Never mind, Curious George," snapped Jody. Throwing him a very un-nice frown, she stuffed her leaflet into her desk. Amanda said nothing, but she did the same.

"For the third time, everyone please look at the board!" Miss Welgloss's voice, stuffed up by her allergies, was short-tempered. "What's the matter with you this morning? Maybe your ears are clogged up, like mine. But I'm warning you all, this is not the day to try my patience. I don't have much of it. All right, who can think of some words with this prefix, *i-n*?" She pointed to a syllable written on the chalkboard.

"Infiltrate," said Marvin.

Someone in the back of the room groaned. Gwen sighed. "Good grief."

"I only want words you can use in a sentence," said the teacher sharply.

"Okay. The enemy spies infiltrated the—the classroom." Grinning, Marvin looked around for approval.

Miss Welgloss smiled in spite of herself as she wrote Marvin's word on the board. "Not bad, Marvin. That makes school life seem a little more interesting than usual, doesn't it?"

But Maureen didn't smile. Her heart was beating fast. What exactly had Marvin meant by that? What did he know? Was he going to tell the teacher anything about the leaflets? She looked searchingly at him, but he met her gaze blandly, as if he had only been fooling around. Maybe he had.

For the rest of the school day everyone seemed to be on edge. Miss Welgloss kept her word about her short temper, criticizing and scolding in a way that wasn't like her at all. And none of the girls were in a good mood, either. At recess they couldn't even agree on what games to play. They stood around for the longest time, giving each other suspicious glances and arguing.

Maureen wondered if Mr. Costue had intended for his leaflets to make everyone unhappy. But it was for their own good, she told herself. Mr. Costue wanted them to have friend insurance in case they lost a friend. And at the rate things were going, it seemed certain that some friends were going to be lost.

But Maureen was ahead of the game! What if her new friend was waiting at home for her right now? She wished the day would go faster.

When Maureen rushed home after school, though, there was no one in the house except her mother, studying as usual in her basement office. Alison wasn't even home, having gone to a friend's house to play.

Maureen didn't mind having a little time before her new friend arrived. That gave her a chance to plan what they could do together. This afternoon, Maureen decided, they would color and set up the cardboard model of Marie Antoinette's palace rooms that her aunt had sent her for Christmas. It was a wonderfully detailed model, the kind of thing Maureen liked to work on, but not by herself. Tracey had never wanted to do it.

After setting out the model and the box of felt pens on her desk, Maureen wandered outside. It was a humid afternoon, with dark clouds hanging over the horse chestnut trees. Where was Maureen's friend?

Would she just show up, or would Mr. Costue deliver her?

What if he had delivered her to the wrong address? That was an awful thought. Maureen walked up the street a few houses, peering into backyards, and then down a few more houses. She saw some younger kids playing outside, but no one her own age.

Turning into her driveway again, Maureen wondered whether she should call Mr. Costue. Could he have forgotten? "Trust me," he had said.

A warm damp wind rustled the leaves on the trees like a restless breathing. Maureen walked up and down the driveway. She sat down on the stone wall beside the driveway, then got up again. If her friend didn't appear by the time she walked up and down the driveway one more time, she would call Mr. Costue's office.

Thunder rumbled in the distance. It's going to rain, thought Maureen. Feeling a pinprick on her arm, she slapped at a mosquito. She reached the end of the driveway, turned and started to walk back.

And then she heard an engine behind her and whirled to see a pink van turning in her driveway. "Mr. Costue?" For a moment she wasn't sure, in spite of the driver's ruddy face and silver mustache. The sympathetic man Maureen had talked to yesterday couldn't have that look on his face—as if he would run down anyone who got in his way.

Then the man's pale blue eyes met hers, and in an instant the first impression was washed away by his smile. "Hi, there!" As he pulled the van up beside Maureen, she noticed the double twisted ribbon insignia on the side. "How are you today, Maureen?"

Maureen saw that there was no one sitting in the seat beside Mr. Costue. "Fine. . . ." Surely her new friend couldn't be in the back of the van. "But where . . . I thought you said . . ."

The friend insurance man grinned at her and swung down from the van. "Patience, patience." Pulling on a pair of work gloves, he asked as if he were making conversation, "Is your mother home, by any chance, Maureen?"

"Yes, but—" Anxiously Maureen shoved her hands into her pockets. Mr. Costue didn't want to talk to her mother, did he? That might spoil everything. "She's studying in the basement, but she gets mad if you interrupt her."

Mr. Costue nodded, his eyes twinkling. "Then we just won't interrupt her, will we, Maureen?"

Of course Mr. Costue knew better than to get her mother involved in this. Maureen followed him around to the back of the van, shivering with excitement. The air seemed to be pressing in on her. Maybe that was just the storm coming on.

Watching Mr. Costue open the back doors of the van, Maureen caught her breath . . . and let it out again in disappointment. The van was filled with tools and equipment, like an electrician's. Mr. Costue pulled out an aluminum extension ladder. Maureen noticed the van's license plate: FRIEND. Well, that made sense. But where *was* her friend?

"Mr. Costue, er . . ." Maureen's voice trailed off at the hard, set expression that had come over the insurance man's face. Buckling a tool belt around his thick waist, he didn't seem to hear her.

He leaned into the van and took out a black plastic-covered object about the size and shape of a round margarine carton. Two prongs, like the plug on the end of a lamp cord, stuck out from the flat side.

"What's that?" asked Maureen.

"The transformer," said Mr. Costue curtly. He dropped it into a pocket of his tool belt. Hoisting the ladder to his shoulder, he carried it up the garden steps to the corner of the house.

Maureen followed him up the steps. Probably Mr. Costue didn't like to be disturbed when he was working. She shouldn't ask any more questions. But what was he doing?

Mr. Costue extended the ladder as far as it would go and leaned it against the house, so that its top rested just below the point where the thick black power lines connected to the house. Maureen stood watching as he mounted the ladder.

Working swiftly with wire strippers and pliers and other tools Maureen didn't know, Mr. Costue attached the black thing—the transformer—to the power lines. Maureen moved uneasily. "Mr. Costue . . . that black thing won't do anything to the electricity, will it? If the

lights go off in Mom's office, she'll be really mad."

"No problem," said Mr. Costue absently. He was climbing down the ladder, sliding it back together. "Now to call Fader." Carrying the ladder down to the van, he jumped into the driver's seat and picked up a telephone on the dashboard. "All set at this end, Fader. Feed the program into the computer. Age ten."

Maureen's breathing was shallow. Without knowing what she was afraid of, she had an impulse to run into the basement and call her mother.

Then Maureen thought she heard a sound from the house. A small explosion, like a baked potato bursting in the oven. Gasping, she turned to Mr. Costue. "What was that?"

But the salesman didn't look worried. In fact, he was beaming now. "There we go!" His face shining pinker than ever, he started the van. "I bet you'll be very pleased with your new friend, Maureen. You can be sure she'll always like you, no matter what." He smiled at her as if it made him happy just to think how happy she would be.

"But—" Maureen trotted alongside the van as Mr. Costue backed down the driveway. "Where—?"

"Just give me a buzz if any problems come up. Our phone number's on your policy." Then, staring at the rearview mirror as if he saw something wonderful, he murmured to himself, "Today, Rushfield; tomorrow, the world!"

"What did you say?" panted Maureen. But with a final wave, Mr. Costue swung the van into the street and disappeared around the curve of Chestnut Hill Road. Maureen stood staring at the end of the driveway as though the pink van with its license plate, FRIEND, were still there.

And then Maureen heard a sound from the other end of the driveway, and turned to see one of the garage doors trembling. Someone was trying to get out. Those doors were heavy; Maureen could hardly lift them herself.

She should go help . . . whoever it was. The doors were easier to open from the outside. But something kept Maureen rooted to the spot as the garage door moved slowly, jerkily up.

Kitty

For a moment Maureen thought the barefoot girl standing in the garage doorway was Alison, and she felt a thud of disappointment. But then she saw that the girl only looked like Alison, with her deep-set eyes and light brown hair. She was taller than Alison, and her hair was pulled back into a pony tail.

Maureen took a few steps down the driveway toward the girl, then a few more. She was so excited that she almost felt sick. This was like Christmas morning times ten, and she was getting just what she had asked for: a new friend. How had Mr. Costue done it?

But she didn't need to know; the important thing was, here was her new friend, blinking and holding up the waistband of her skirt with one hand. Why did she have to hold up her skirt? Never mind that now!

"Hi." Her voice was shaky. "I'm Maureen Harrity."

Smoothing wisps of hair back from her face, the other girl frowned and squinted into the distance as if she was making an effort to remember something. Then she gave up with a shake of her head. "Hello. I'm . . . Kitty."

"Hi," said Maureen again. She didn't know where to begin. Did Kitty know anything about Maureen or Mr. Costue? Where had Kitty come from? How long could she stay? Without knowing those things, it was hard to start talking to her. On the other hand, Maureen hesitated to ask questions. Kitty's appearance was almost like something out of a fairy tale, and in fairy tales the magic melted away when people got too nosy.

"Do you have a safety pin?" asked Kitty finally. She hitched up her skirt to get a better grip on it.

Maureen laughed with relief. People in fairy tales never needed safety pins to hold their skirts up. Kitty was real, all right. "Sure. Come on in—" Feeling a drop of rain on the top of her head, Maureen stopped and looked up. Lightning crackled across the dark clouds. "Come on inside, quick! No, this way," she called as Kitty turned back toward the garage. Maureen didn't want to lead Kitty into the house through the basement, where her mother was studying. She wanted a chance to talk to Kitty and calm down before she had to introduce the other girl to her mother.

With Kitty close behind, Maureen ran up the garden steps to the kitchen door. They stood in the dark kitchen while Maureen tried vainly to switch the light on. "The power must be out." Oh, dear, Mom wouldn't be able to study in her office if the power was out. She would come upstairs.

"Maybe it's just this room," said Kitty briskly. "Let's go down to the basement and see if a switch in the switch box has flipped."

"No!" Maureen added hastily, "I know where there's a safety pin in my room, anyway." But just as she spoke, the overhead light came on. Maureen smiled happily at Kitty, because now her mother would stay in the basement for a while. "Hey, you know what would be better than a safety pin? You could wear something of mine."

"That *would* be better, if you have some long pants and a shirt," agreed Kitty. "It's gotten c-cold all of a sudden." She glanced out the kitchen window at the rain splashing on the deck, and frowned. "Look at the way the water's pouring off the roof. The gutters must be clogged with leaves." She made a *tsk-tsk* sound.

Maureen thought it was odd for Kitty to be concerned about clogged gutters, but she answered, "I guess my father didn't have time to clean the gutters before he went to Montreal. Anyway, it *is* getting cold. Want some cocoa? I'll put the kettle on"—she filled it at the sink—"and it'll be boiling by the time you change your clothes. I love cocoa on rainy days, don't you? It makes me feel cozy." Switching the burner on high, she hugged herself comfortably.

"Cocoa?" Kitty looked as if she were tasting something sickeningly sweet. "Actually . . . could I have coffee instead?"

"Coffee?" Maureen stared at her new friend. Where did Kitty come from, anyway—some far-off land where fifth graders drank coffee? But if that's what Kitty wanted . . . "I guess so." She checked in the cupboard. "Yeah, sure. There's some instant coffee. Well, let's go to my room."

In her bedroom, Maureen pulled a pair of jeans and a red-striped polo shirt from her dresser drawers. "Here, these should fit you all right. They're just a little small for me."

Kitty took the clothes, but she held up the shirt with a look of dissatisfaction. "Red? Don't you have anything else? I think red makes me look washed out."

This seemed like a strange objection, but Maureen opened her shirt drawer again. "Okay. Here's a green one."

"Green is my color." Looking pleased, Kitty reached for the shirt. But then she stretched it out between her hands, examining the front with a frown. "Oh, dear. What's this on the front? It looks like spaghetti sauce. How long has it been there? It should have been washed right away, because it's hard to get stains out once they set."

Good grief, thought Maureen. She hoped Kitty wasn't always so fussy. But she only said, "Okay, I'll put that in the laundry. Here, wear this T-shirt."

On the back, the T-shirt said, I Brake for Junk Food. Kitty looked at it for a moment. Then she said, "I guess I'll take the red-striped one, after all."

As Kitty started to undress, Maureen politely turned her back, in case the other girl was shy. She thought of what Mr. Costue had said, that she would be pleased with her new friend, and wondered if they liked and disliked all the same things. What if Kitty wanted to be on the swim team, like Tracey? "Do you like to swim?" she asked over her shoulder.

"Swimming's all right," said Kitty. "The only trouble is, after you go swimming, you have wet hair."

"I know," said Maureen eagerly. She turned back to Kitty, who was dressed now, with her skirt and blouse folded neatly on Maureen's bed. "It's a pain." She felt more satisfied. Of course Kitty would be the perfect friend for Maureen. It would just take a little while for them to get used to each other, that's all. Kitty would be lots of fun, and very loyal. "She'll always like you, no matter what," Mr. Costue had assured her.

A door slammed in the kitchen, and Alison's voice yelled, "Mauree-een!"

Maureen looked at Kitty, making a face. "That's my dear little sister, Alison. She sounds like a moose, doesn't she?"

"Mauree-een!" Alison blared as she ran down the hall. She stuck her head, stringy-haired from running through the rain, in the door. "Maureen, you'd better turn off the kettle, or it'll boil dry and the spout will

drop off like last time, and Mommy'll be really—" She stopped, gazing at Kitty. "Who's that?"

Maureen started to say, "Don't you have any manners?" but Kitty spoke first. "A better way to introduce yourself," she suggested gently, "might be to say, 'Hello, I'm Alison. What's your name?' "

Maureen and Alison both stared at Kitty. It was an odd joke. Maureen laughed uncomfortably. Kitty *was* joking, wasn't she? What if she turned out to be a goody-goody kind of girl? But Mr. Costue couldn't possibly think that Maureen would want that kind of friend.

"Well!" said Maureen. "Let's go get our cocoa, Kitty. I mean, our cocoa and coffee."

"Coffee?" said Alison, following Maureen and Kitty back down the hall to the kitchen. "Does she drink *coffee*? Does your mother let you?" she asked Kitty.

"Just shush, Alison," said Maureen. She was afraid Kitty might not want to spend much time with her if she was pestered by Alison.

But Kitty had that funny expression on her face again, squinting and frowning a little as if she was trying to remember.

Trying to remember what? Whether her mother would let her drink coffee?

Smoothing her hair back toward her pony tail, Kitty looked vaguely over Alison's shoulder. "I don't think she minds."

"Well, *our* mother would never let us drink coffee."

Alison watched Maureen get two mugs from one cupboard and the instant coffee and cocoa from the other. "Hey, I want some cocoa, too, Maureen. I need it more than you do—I got all wet running into the house."

"There isn't enough." Maureen spooned coffee granules into one mug and began scraping the last of the cocoa mix into the other. "Barely enough for one."

"Meanie!" Alison stuck her hands on her hips. "Mean Maureen, you're so mean I can't believe it. And I'm going to tell Mommy. Mommy!" She started for the basement door.

"Go ahead. *You* ate the last of the ice cream yesterday." Maureen poured boiling water into the mugs. By the time Alison got Mom upstairs, Maureen would have drunk most of the cocoa. "Here's your . . . your coffee, Kitty."

But Kitty put the coffee down on the counter. "Good lord. There's no need for you girls to bicker like this, when there's a perfectly simple solution." As Maureen stood at the stove, stunned, Kitty took the mug of cocoa from her hand. Then Kitty reached another mug down from the cupboard, and held them over the sink to pour half the cocoa into the empty mug. She handed it to Alison. "Now, couldn't you two have thought of that? Really!"

"Thanks, Kitty." Alison sipped her cocoa, looking smug. Half a cup was more than she had expected to get.

Alison probably thinks Kitty likes her, thought

Maureen resentfully. But *I'm* the one she likes. Mr. Costue said so. Unless something had gotten mixed up?

The phone rang, and Maureen picked up the receiver. It was Mrs. Twill, who drove to classes in the city with her mother. "May I speak to Kathleen?"

"She's downstairs. Just a minute, please." Maureen noticed that Kitty and Alison were settling down together at the kitchen table, Kitty stirring cream and sugar into her coffee. What if Kitty was the type of girl who liked younger kids better than kids her own age? The type of girl who couldn't wait to be old enough to baby-sit? Maureen hoped not. Opening the door to the basement stairs, she called down, "Mom! Telephone!"

There was no answer. Mom must be concentrating so hard that she didn't hear. Maureen turned back to look at Kitty, who seemed to be listening with interest to Alison's chatter. "And what else happened today at school?" she was asking.

Frowning, Maureen clattered down the steps to the basement. "Mom!" she yelled. "Mom . . ."

At the bottom of the basement steps Maureen paused, wrinkling her nose. There was an unpleasant smell in the basement, something like the way the kitchen smelled if Mom was cracking eggs into the frying pan and let strands of egg white fall on the burner. Ugh!

But Mom couldn't be frying eggs down here.

Holding her nose, Maureen walked over to her mother's office and pushed open the door. "Mom—"

Her mother was not in the office.

But the smell was. And something dark—brown drops, Maureen saw as she peered closer—had spattered over her book and notebook and desk. Brown puddles splotched the cement floor around the chair. A few droplets even speckled the wall near the desk.

"Mom!" Maureen tried to scream, but as if she were in a nightmare, the scream wouldn't come out of her throat. She choked on the burned egg-white smell.

For a moment Maureen stood there trembling, her mind blank. And then, one after another, the facts lined up in her mind:

Kitty had appeared out of the garage—out of the basement, really. That was where the explosion noise had come from.

Kitty had deep-set eyes and a habit of smoothing back her light brown hair. And her skirt had been falling off her because it was big enough for a grown-up woman. And she had wanted coffee instead of cocoa, and she had corrected Alison's and Maureen's manners.

Maureen had sent Costue and Fader a hair from her mother with the Friend Loss Report. Part of her mother, with all the information for her mother in its cells, as Marvin had said.

"Is your mother home?" Mr. Costue had asked.

Mr. Costue! Maureen had to get hold of him right away, tell him that wasn't what she had wanted, that he had to—had to—

Desperately Maureen pushed back the question of whether Mr. Costue could do anything, now. She stepped back, pulling the office door shut. Costue and Fader *had* to . . . fix things up again. It was a terrible mistake, a terrible misunderstanding. Mr. Costue had meant to help Maureen, but he had done just the opposite. How could someone who seemed as understanding as Mr. Costue be so mistaken?

A horrifying thought occurred to Maureen. Maybe she had somehow given Mr. Costue the impression that she knew how he was going to get her a new friend, and that she wanted him to do it!

With a moan Maureen dashed up the basement stairs two at a time. But at the door into the kitchen she stopped short, hearing Alison's chattering and Kitty's patient answers. She couldn't face that—that person who called herself Kitty. It was too horrible. She would run into her parents' bedroom and call Costue and Fader from the extension phone.

Phone. Mrs. Twill was waiting on the phone to talk to her mother! Maureen couldn't call the insurance company until the line was free. Taking a deep breath, Maureen strode across the kitchen to the telephone. From the corner of her eye she saw that Kitty and Alison were still sitting at the kitchen table, sipping from their mugs. "Do you like to play Sorry?" Alison was asking. Maureen didn't dare look at them.

Clutching the counter for support, Maureen spoke shakily into the receiver. "My mother can't come to the phone right now. Can I—" Then she noticed the dial tone humming in her ear. Mrs. Twill must have gotten tired of waiting and hung up. Thank goodness!

Carefully Maureen replaced the receiver, carefully she stepped across the kitchen floor, still not looking at Kitty or Alison. "Back in a minute," she said over her shoulder, trying to sound casual. Then she stumbled down the hall to her room. Mr. Costue said the telephone number for Costue and Fader was on the Friend Insurance Policy. The policy was in her desk drawer. Yes. Picking up the policy, Maureen lurched out of her room toward her parents' bedroom.

At the door of their room Maureen paused, her heart jumping with a wild hope. Maybe she was completely mistaken, getting all upset for nothing. Maybe the brown stuff was spilled coffee. Maybe her mother had come upstairs so quietly that no one had noticed. Maybe she was in her bedroom right now, or in her bathroom. . . .

The bedroom was empty. In a glance Maureen took in the open bathroom door, the open closets, the dresser with her mother's purse lying on it. Sinking down on the bed beside the night table, she picked up the telephone. "Just give me a buzz if any problems

61

come up," Mr. Costue had said. Maureen let out a bitter laugh that turned into a sob.

Forcing her fingers to stop shaking, she dialed the phone number on the policy.

It's Up to You, Maureen

"Hello," mumbled a man's voice, so low Maureen could hardly hear him.

"Mr. Costue!" Maureen's own voice was choked. "My mother—she's—"

"Oh, dear," said the man. "Mr. Costue isn't here, and I can't remember exactly what he told me to say. But there's no reason to be upset."

Maureen, who had been all set to pour out her story to Mr. Costue, could hardly keep from bursting into tears. "Mr. Costue isn't there?"

"No." The man paused, and then he went on in a rapid, nervous way, "I wish Will *were* here. He's much better at talking to people. I'm shy. I try not to be, but I can't help it. Mr. Costue went to pick up the pizza. Maybe he'll call you back. But he has to do what he thinks best. He understands these things much better than I do."

Maureen didn't know what to do. This must be Mr. Fader, that droopy man she had seen in the back of the office. She didn't want to talk to him, but she couldn't hang up. She couldn't wait. "I have to talk to Mr. Costue right away," she said, trying to keep her voice calm. "I asked for a friend, but I didn't expect Mr. Costue to turn my mother into a girl. That was crazy! That was very—dangerous!" The last word made her gulp.

"Dangerous?" Mr. Fader sounded amazed. "Oh, no, no. You're mistaken there. My method of turning back the biological clock is quite safe—as safe as can be." His tone shifted from nervous to authoritative. "I know I'm not good at talking to people, but I am a serious scientist, a molecular biologist, and I would never dream of applying experimental methods to human subjects. You can rest assured that I tested my procedure on dozens of white rats before I even thought of using it on a human being."

"White rats! But my mother is not a white rat!" Maureen was trembling. "Why did you have to do it to her at all? Why couldn't you just make a new friend for me, if you're such a great scientist?"

"I wish Will were here," said Mr. Fader plaintively. "He explains things so much better than I can. . . . Well, let me try. When I started this line of research, I *thought* I could grow human clones, using the information in the DNA molecule (the secret of life itself, you know) and a bathtub full of lemon gelatin, plus a sprinkling of other ingredients. But I guess I was overly optimistic. However, I did make another important breakthrough, the discovery of how to turn a person's biological clock backward. And then I met Will Costue (he's a genius, isn't he?) and he suggested that he and I, working together, could use my discovery for the benefit of all."

"Benefit!" Maureen was beginning to hate this man. "Some benefit. If you don't—"

"Just a minute," interrupted Mr. Fader. He sounded relieved. "Will's coming in right now. He explains things so much better. Here he is."

Maureen barely heard, "Get back to the computer." Then, in a louder and quite a different tone, "Maureen." Mr. Costue's rich, warm voice seemed to pour through the phone into Maureen's ear. "Good to hear from you! How are things going?"

Immediately Maureen felt better. Mr. Costue would straighten things out. Probably Mr. Fader, who sounded like some kind of crackpot, had made a mistake. "Please, Mr. Costue, you've got to come and change my mother back, right away!"

There was silence on the other end. Then Mr. Costue spoke in an astonished tone. "You don't like your new friend? Well, well! I thought she would be just what you asked for."

"But—" Now Maureen was astonished. "Kitty? I—

65

I guess she's all right. But now I don't . . . I don't have my mother!"

"But . . . I'm not sure what the problem is, Maureen." Mr. Costue sounded genuinely puzzled.

Maureen swallowed a sob. "I need my mother! Oh, Mr. Costue, don't you understand that?"

"Of course." Mr. Costue's voice flowed out of the phone like honey. "Of course you do, generally speaking. But which do you need more right now—your mother, or a good friend?" His voice took on a hurt tone, as if Maureen were accusing him unjustly. "I thought, from your enthusiasm about friend insurance, that you needed a friend more than anything, Maureen."

Baffled, Maureen bunched up the coiled telephone cord with one hand. It wound around itself, like the twisted ribbons sign on the side of Mr. Costue's van. "I do. But—I can't get along without my mother." She was beginning to feel frightened again. Why didn't he seem to understand?

"Mm, perhaps," said Mr. Costue, as if he wasn't at all convinced. "But don't you think you could get along without your mother just for a day or two? A mature girl like yourself? And in the meantime, Maureen, we'll work on other friend arrangements for you."

Maureen was so surprised that she said nothing for a moment, letting the idea sink in. "But my father's away, and I'm not old enough to stay overnight by

myself," she said finally. But even as she spoke, she knew it wasn't true. Of course Mom and Dad would never leave her overnight. But if they did, she and Alison would be fine. They could fix themselves something to eat, put themselves to bed, get themselves off to school in the morning. Mr. Costue was right.

Maureen frowned. Somehow she was getting off the track. She hadn't even asked the most important question. "But my mother—*can* you change her back again?"

"My goodness!" Mr. Costue's jolly laugh crackled in her ear. "You thought—my goodness, no wonder you were upset. I didn't get it! Of course we can reverse the development. We still have your friend's DNA code in our data bank, and the transformer is still hooked up to your power lines, I assume. So of course we can reverse. And then you'll be back to square one —with a mother, but no friend. Just say the word. Right now, if you like." Mr. Costue paused. Then, with a sad note in his voice, he asked, "Or would you like to say good-bye to your new friend first?"

"I—" Maureen hesitated. She thought of tomorrow, when she would have to go to school again and face Tracey and Gwen. Without a best friend. Back to square one. Or . . . she could go to school with Kitty.

After all, how could it hurt to keep Kitty overnight, for one day? Mr. Costue was so right—at the moment she needed a friend much more than she needed a mother. "Well . . ."

"Or would you like to keep your friend for another hour or so?" Mr. Costue sounded eager to do whatever she wanted. "It's up to you, Maureen."

Maureen felt a little foolish. She had made such a fuss, when there was really nothing the matter. Of course she couldn't keep her mother for a best friend very long, but why shouldn't she keep Kitty overnight, and take her to school tomorrow? Why shouldn't she keep her until Friday, so she would have a partner on the field trip? "What if—what if I had Kitty stay until Friday afternoon? Would that be all right?"

"Absolutely fine," said Mr. Costue heartily. "It's entirely up to you. Just give us a buzz, then. Oh—one more thing, Maureen. Did you manage to hand out those leaflets I gave you?"

"Yes, I did," answered Maureen proudly. "I gave one to every girl in my class."

"Excellent, Maureen!" Mr. Costue sounded excited. "And they'll have gotten the report forms in the mail this afternoon. Excellent timing. I knew I could count on you."

"But, Mr. Costue . . ." Maureen remembered how disturbing the leaflets had been to Tracey and Gwen and Jody and Amanda and the other girls in her class. "I'm not so sure friend insurance is a good idea for these other kids. The leaflets made them feel terrible."

"Well, Maureen"—Mr. Costue sighed—"the truth isn't always pretty. But people have to face the truth, don't you think? Then they can take steps to help themselves. Of course you're a sensitive and caring person, and you don't like to see others upset. But it's for their own good. Well, it's been great talking to you, Maureen. Good-bye."

Hanging up the phone, Maureen let out a shaky sigh. So everything was all right. Mr. Costue could change Kitty back any time she asked. And there was no reason to give up Kitty right away. Dad didn't have to know anything, because he was in Montreal until Saturday. Alison—Maureen would have to think up something to tell Alison. She would tell her that Mom had to go away suddenly. To Aunt Marcia's, in New Hampshire?

Yes. That would be a good story. Maureen stood up, feeling her legs a little unsteady. Folding the insurance policy and sticking it into her pocket, she walked slowly back down the hall to the kitchen.

Maureen felt slightly superior, hearing Alison chattering away to Kitty. Of course Alison didn't know what Maureen knew, but didn't she find anything strange about a fifth-grade girl's being so interested in her friend's little sister? Alison probably thought it was because of her own delightful personality.

Maureen had to admit, though, that no one would suspect the truth at first glance. Kitty certainly seemed to be a girl Maureen's age—a girl who looked a lot like Alison, true, but you couldn't expect Alison to notice that.

"Kitty wants to play Sorry with me," said Alison in a pleased tone. "Want to play too, Maureen?"

"Not really," said Maureen. If Kitty was only going to be here two days, Maureen wanted to start the model of Marie Antoinette's rooms right away. "Kitty, you don't have to do everything Alison wants just to be nice."

Kitty winked over Alison's head, as if to say that the two older girls could afford to humor Alison. "Oh, come on, Maureen. Just one game."

Maureen was about to argue when the phone rang again, and she picked it up. "Hello? . . . Oh."

It was Mrs. Twill, with a sharp note in her voice now. "I thought someone was going to get your mother. I finally hung up and called again, and then the line was busy for *quite* a long time."

Maureen had forgotten all about her. "Oh, I'm awfully sorry."

"Do you think I could talk to your mother now?"

Maureen blushed. "Sure. Oh—I mean, I'm afraid she went out. I thought she was home, but I guess she went out for a walk or something." (In the pouring rain?) "Can I take a message?"

"Yes . . ." She sounded doubtful that Maureen was responsible enough. "Do you have a pencil? Please tell her Nancy Twill—*T-w-i-l-l*— called, and she doesn't need to pick me up in the morning, because I won't be able to go to class tomorrow. But I'll pick her up Friday, as usual. All right? Now, you won't forget to give her the message, will you? Thank you very much."

"Thank *you*," breathed Maureen. That was a lucky escape! She hadn't even thought about Mom's car pool with Mrs. Twill. They drove into the city to their classes on Thursdays and Fridays. If Mrs. Twill had waited for Mom to pick her up tomorrow and Mom never came, there would have been a lot of trouble.

Maureen looked down at the message she had written on the note pad. Tearing it off, she stuck it in her pocket. Mom wouldn't need that, but Maureen would, because tomorrow she would have to call Mrs. Twill back with some excuse for Friday morning, when Kitty would be on the field trip with Maureen and Kathleen Harrity would have to have a touch of the flu, or something.

Turning away from the phone, Maureen had an inspiration. Alison was in the family room with Kitty, setting up the Sorry game. She hadn't heard the conversation, and didn't know who Maureen had been talking to. Maureen strolled into the family room and sat down on the carpet with the other girls. "Guess who that was on the phone? Mom."

Alison looked up at her. "Mommy?" She laughed disbelievingly. "Come on. She's downstairs."

Maureen noticed that Kitty was gazing from Maureen to Alison, a little line appearing between her eyebrows. But she went on, "I thought she was downstairs, too, but she said she left a while ago, when I was out for a walk. See, Aunt Marcia's in terrible trouble, and she called Mom from New Hampshire and asked her to come right away."

"What kind of trouble?"

"I don't know." Maureen felt a thrill of excitement. Yes, Alison might believe her, if she could just act normal. "It must be something really bad, because Mom wouldn't tell me. But anyway, she's going to have to stay up there tonight and help Aunt Marcia take care of the twins, and stuff like that. She'll be back tomorrow . . . or the day after."

"Oh," said Alison, still looking puzzled. "Why didn't she tell you before she left?"

"Because I wasn't here, and she was in a big hurry." The explanation rolled smoothly from Maureen's lips.

"But—" A whine came into Alison's voice, and her lower lip quivered. "Who's going to take care of us? Daddy isn't even here!"

Maureen made her voice as offhand as possible. "Oh, Mom thought we would be okay on our own. She— she left some money so I could buy groceries." Maureen thought of the purse on her mother's dresser, and hoped there really was some money in it. "And she said we could scrape something up for dinner tonight. There's soup and stuff in the cupboard." Maureen was pretty sure this was true.

Fiddling with one of the Sorry pieces, Kitty pressed her lips together. "I don't think it's wise to let you and Alison stay by yourselves. What if the power went off again, for longer than it did this afternoon? Or what if there was a medical emergency, and someone needed to be driven to the hospital? There ought to be an adult in the house for things like that."

Maureen noticed with annoyance that Alison's lower lip was trembling again. "Nothing like that is going to happen," she said firmly. "And if it did, we could always call the neighbors." She had another thought and went on boldly, "I told Mom you were here, Kitty, and she said that was good, because you could stay overnight and keep me company and help take care of Alison."

"I can take care of myself." Alison sat up straight. Then she added, "*Can* you stay over, Kitty? Why don't you call your mother and ask?"

Kitty stared down at the game board, looking confused and unhappy. Smoothing her hair back, she started to speak, then stopped, as if it was simply impossible to answer Alison's question.

Again Maureen felt a surge of excitement. It was working! Things were going the way she wanted them to. "I'm *sure* it will be all right for Kitty to stay over," she said. She imagined Kitty calling up Grandma in Ohio and asking, "Can I sleep over at Maureen's?" A high-pitched giggle formed at the back of her throat, but she choked it down.

Still staring at the Sorry board, Kitty said in a dazed way, "Yes . . . I'm sure it will be all right."

Maureen Takes Charge

As it turned out, they played not one, but *three* games of Sorry, and Alison won them all, mostly because Kitty helped her. "It's just a game of luck" said Maureen, trying not to sound spiteful. When Mr. Costue said her new friend would always like her no matter what, he hadn't mentioned that her new friend would also be a pushover for her little sister.

To Maureen's relief Alison was hungry and ready to quit after the third game. "I'm hungry, too," said Kitty as they trooped into the kitchen to see what there was for supper. She peered into the sparsely filled refrigerator. "Someone should have gone grocery shopping."

"*We* can go shopping tomorrow after school." Maureen thought that she should check her mother's purse as soon as she got a chance. "Tonight we can have soup, and cheese and crackers."

"That's a yucky supper," said Alison. "I wish Mommy was here."

"And a delicious dessert," continued Maureen brightly, opening the cupboard. "How about—" Her eye rested on a package of lemon gelatin, and she was about to suggest that, but then she remembered that gelatin took a long time to set.

"How about chocolate chips?" Without even looking, Kitty plunged her hand into the cupboard up to her shoulder, and pulled a whole bag of chocolate chips out from behind the soup cans.

Alison laughed delightedly. "Kitty! How did you know they were there? Your mother must hide them in the same place."

Kitty didn't say anything, and neither did Maureen.

After supper Kitty picked up the evening newspaper and said firmly, "I'd like some time to myself, now." Maureen and Alison watched her stroll into the family room and settle herself on the sofa with her legs crossed.

Maureen felt Alison's questioning look, but she refused to meet it. "Aren't you supposed to take a bath tonight, Alison?" she asked to distract her.

But Alison was not to be distracted. "What's the

matter with Kitty?" she whispered loudly. "I mean, she's nice, but— Is she sort of—you know—cuckoo?" She looked more interested than worried.

"Shush." Nodding warningly toward the family room, Maureen beckoned Alison down the hall. Should she tell Alison the truth? It might be easier.

No, no! Alison would have a fit. Maureen bent down toward her sister's ear. "I'll tell you, but don't say anything about it to Kitty."

Alison nodded, her mouth open.

"Kitty's a genius. That means, she's very, very smart. So sometimes she acts different from other kids. But it's just because she thinks all the time. She'll probably be very famous when she grows up."

"Oh." Alison looked pleased and excited. "*That's* why she's sort of weird."

"Yes. Anyway," said Maureen, "you'd better go take your bath now."

Maureen was just as glad to have some time to herself, too, to plan for tomorrow. Kitty would go to school with Maureen. She would introduce Kitty to Miss Welgloss as her friend visiting from—New Hampshire? And she would tell the teacher that Kitty would be her partner on the field trip.

Reminded of the field trip, Maureen got the permission slip out of her book bag. Oh, dear. Why hadn't she gotten Mom to sign it? Maureen was supposed to turn it in tomorrow morning.

Maureen would just have to sign it herself. Taking the slip into her parents' bedroom, she got her mother's wallet out of her purse and looked at the signature on her driver's license. Signing someone else's name was forgery, Maureen knew.

Still, Mom certainly would have signed it, if she could have. Maureen was just doing it for her. That wasn't really forgery. Grasping the pen firmly, Maureen scrawled *Kathleen M. Harrity* at the bottom of the permission slip. It wasn't exactly like her mother's writing, but that didn't matter. Miss Welgloss wouldn't know. The main thing was that it looked messy, like grown-up handwriting.

Then Maureen checked the money in her mother's wallet. About twenty dollars—plenty to get a few groceries tomorrow. She and Kitty could ride bikes to the A&P.

When Maureen went back to the family room, she was wondering whether Kitty would want to stay up late, and what Alison would think of that. But Kitty was yawning and stretching on the sofa. "It's early, but for some reason I'm exhausted." She borrowed a nightgown from Maureen.

"I wish Mommy was here," whimpered Alison, pink and damp from her bath. "She shouldn't have left us all alone. I'm scared. I want to call her up."

Maureen swallowed a gasp. Calling up Mom at Aunt Marcia's was one thing Alison mustn't do. "Mom said we shouldn't. It's long distance, and it costs a lot." Then Maureen had the brilliant idea that they could all sleep together in her parents' bed. Alison seemed satisfied, tucked in on the other side of Kitty, hugging her teddy bear.

As Maureen reached out to turn off the lamp, Kitty leaned over and kissed Alison good-night. Maureen saw what was coming and braced herself. "Good night, dear," said Kitty, planting a kiss on Maureen's cheek.

" 'Night," muttered Maureen. She tried not to squirm. It was just so—so *strange*, even if she did know why Kitty was doing it.

Now that Maureen was lying in bed in the dark, no longer busy making plans, it occurred to her that friend insurance had not worked out the way she expected. She had expected to be supplied with a wonderful lifetime friend, but what she had actually gotten was a peculiar friend, on loan for a couple of days.

Of course Mr. Costue had said that in the meantime he would "work on other friend arrangements." Maureen felt sure that he wouldn't leave her in the lurch when he changed Kitty back, quite sure. . . .

"Maureen."

Who had said that? Maureen's eyes opened to a still dark room. Someone had spoken in her ear. Or was it a dream?

Groggily Maureen pushed herself up on one elbow.

She was not in her own bed. In the dark she could barely see two other heads on the pillows. She must have had a nightmare, and climbed into bed with Mom and Dad. But—

No. She sat up in bed, a chill running over her. Now she remembered. Those other heads were Alison and . . . Kitty.

Maureen felt hollow. What had she done? She stared around the room at the gray and black shadows. 3:06, said the red-numbered clock on the other side of the bed.

Yesterday afternoon, when Maureen was talking to Mr. Costue on the phone, it had seemed all right to keep Kitty for another day or so. But now Maureen was frightened. She seemed to see the twisted ribbons from Mr. Costue's leaflet dangling before her, only they were joined by links like ladder rungs, because—

She felt a jolt as two separate things clapped together in her mind: the twisted ribbons insignia and Marvin's DNA molecule model. No, it wasn't a coincidence! Mr. Fader had mentioned DNA, too. "The secret of life itself."

Why had Mr. Costue told her the insignia was a symbol of friendship? Why hadn't he told her the truth?

Maureen was shivering, and her breathing was rapid and shallow. Calm down, Maureen told herself sternly. She was flying off the handle, the way she had done when she found the—the mess in her mother's office.

80

That mess. That was what was really bothering her. All evening she had managed to forget about it, but now she gasped, remembering the brown drops spattered over the desk and floor and wall. She couldn't leave it like that. What if Alison went down to the basement? Maureen had better go clean it up, right now.

Slipping out of bed, Maureen replaced the covers carefully so that Kitty wouldn't wake up. But the other girl stirred in her sleep, muttering.

Maureen froze, bent over the bed. What had she said?

Flinging an arm outside the covers, Kitty pulled them up to her chin. "Maureen, why don't you ask someone else . . . ?" Her voice died away in a murmur.

Maureen sucked in her breath, straining her eyes to see if Kitty was awake. For several moments she stood there, waiting and watching. But as the covers rose and fell slowly over Kitty and Alison, Maureen's heartbeat slowed to normal. With one last backward glance, she tiptoed out of her parents' bedroom and down the hall to the kitchen.

Taking the whole roll of paper towels and the bottle of spray cleaner, Maureen padded down the basement stairs to her mother's office. She walked more and more slowly as she came up to the door. The burned egg-white smell was faint, but still there. Her stomach felt queasy.

Maureen took a deep breath, pushed open the door,

and turned on the light. Not giving herself time to think, she sprayed at the brown splotches on the floor, dropped to her knees, and began scrubbing under the desk. The brown stuff had dried. But with a couple more squirts of the spray, it began to dissolve and wipe off on the paper towels.

Then she turned to clean the walls. The drops on the paneling came off more easily, thank goodness. Now the desk . . . The brown specks on the pages of her mother's notebook and textbook wouldn't come off, of course. Maureen just shut the books and pushed them into the bookshelf behind the desk.

There. She had wiped up every brown spot in the office, and now it smelled like spray cleaner instead of burned egg white. Maureen was surprised at how satisfied she felt.

Turning off the light, she climbed back up the stairs. She stuffed the dirty paper towels and empty spray cleaner bottle into the trash basket under the kitchen sink. Now there was nothing for Alison to find.

No, wait. Maureen paused outside her bedroom door. There were her mother's skirt and blouse, on the bed where Kitty had left them. Alison hadn't noticed them that afternoon, but only by luck. Maureen bunched up the skirt and blouse, and poked the clothes into the laundry hamper in the hall.

There! She had thought of everything. Tiptoeing into her parents' bedroom, Maureen crawled back into bed beside Kitty. There was nothing to worry about.

After all, Mom was right here, even if she was in a different shape.

And actually there was no reason to feel so guilty about letting Mom stay Maureen's age for a day or two. Wasn't that what grown-ups always said they wanted —to be young again? Maybe Maureen was doing Mom a favor. True, Kitty didn't seem to be enjoying herself much yet, but probably she would loosen up soon. She would stop acting so much like a mother and start having a good time being ten again.

Maureen snuggled up to Kitty until her bent knees fit into the backs of Kitty's knees. Now she could sleep soundly, looking forward to a day at school with her new friend.

Trouble with "Clones"

At school that morning, Maureen brought a chair from the back of the room so that Kitty could sit beside her desk. She was a little nervous about introducing Kitty to Jody and Amanda as her friend from New Hampshire, but they seemed to believe her. Kitty looked dazed and confused again, although she didn't deny what Maureen said.

Maureen noticed with satisfaction that Tracey was staring at Kitty, her dark eyes glinting. Hah-hah to Tracey, who thought Maureen would be standing by as her second-best friend! Maureen didn't see any need to introduce Kitty to Tracey or Gwen.

While Miss Welgloss took attendance, the boys and girls settled into their seats. A folded pink paper slipped out of Jody's pocket, falling into the aisle. Jody didn't notice, but Maureen did. Jody's Friend Loss Report! Was she thinking of turning it in?

Maureen was about to say something to her when Marvin, who sat behind Jody, swung forward and picked up the paper. As he unfolded it, he merely looked curious. But then his eyes began to run over the report, and he drew in his breath sharply.

Nudged by Maureen, Jody whirled around in her seat and grabbed the pink paper from Marvin. "Give me that!"

"No, wait." Marvin's face was serious; Maureen could see that he wasn't trying to tease Jody. "Where'd you get that? You got it from that Santa Claus clone who was here Tuesday, didn't you?" His whisper became urgent. "You aren't going to give him those hairs, are you? Do you know what's going on?"

Hastily refolding the pink paper, Jody stuffed it back into her pocket. "This is *none* of your business, Marvin! Just mind your own business!" Her face was red right up to her straight bangs, and she didn't look at either Amanda, who was leaning forward trying to hear, or Maureen.

"Look, Jody, I'm not being nosy, really." Speaking earnestly, Marvin stooped in the aisle beside Jody's desk. "Don't you see what's going on? It's a clone plot, like in *Invasion of the Body Snatchers*. Did you see that movie on TV last week? These plants from outer space were growing clones to take the places of people!"

Jody's face was still red, but she laughed a little in

spite of herself. "*Mar*vin. Do you believe all that science fiction stuff? This isn't anything like plants from outer space. It's like—like computer dating. Go sit down and stop bothering me."

"Yeah!" Marvin didn't budge. "Computers—that's how *these* clones are doing it. They're getting people to give them the DNA information, and then they'll sort out all the information in computers and replace the people with clones."

On the other side of Maureen, Kitty put a hand on her arm. "Why are those children talking? Didn't they hear the bell ring?"

Maureen threw Kitty a forced smile. "Oh, it's just a silly argument." She had been feeling more and more uncomfortable, listening to Marvin. Of course he had it all wrong. There wasn't any plot. Still, he was close enough to the truth—too close. And Maureen didn't like the idea, somehow, of Jody turning her Friend Loss Report in to Costue and Fader. What if the same thing happened to Jody that had happened to Maureen? Maureen had handled it all right, but not everyone was as mature as she was, as Mr. Costue had pointed out. Jody might be terribly upset. Should Maureen warn her?

Miss Welgloss's stuffed-up voice cut into Maureen's thoughts. "Marvin, into your seat, please! The bell has rung."

Maureen looked anxiously at Marvin. Was he going to tell Miss Welgloss about the "clone plot"? The teacher wouldn't believe him, of course, but she might ask to see Jody's Friend Loss Report. Then, who knew what might happen?

Marvin hesitated beside Jody's desk, an indignant look on his face. He seemed almost about to say something—and then he closed his mouth and sat down.

Maureen let out a long sigh. Marvin must have realized that Miss Welgloss wouldn't believe that science fiction stuff, either.

Taking a tissue from her skirt pocket, Miss Welgloss wiped her nose. "Before we get into reading, let's have your permission slips for the field trip tomorrow. Maureen, please collect the slips. Who remembered to bring them in?"

Only a few boys and girls raised their hands. Maureen took her own signed permission slip from her book bag, congratulating herself for remembering it in spite of everything that had happened since yesterday afternoon. "Come on up with me," she whispered to Kitty. "I'll introduce you to Miss Welgloss."

The teacher smiled at Kitty, shaking her hand. "It's nice to have you with us, Kitty. Does your school in New Hampshire get out early, or are you just taking a vacation?"

Maureen saw that unhappy, confused look gathering in Kitty's eyes. "Her school gets out very early," she said hastily. "Do you think it would be all right for Kitty to go on the field trip tomorrow? She would be my partner."

Miss Welgloss nodded. "Fine, but I'll need a permission slip for her, too." She handed Maureen a blank slip. "And don't forget to bring it in tomorrow, or she won't be able to come with us." In a louder voice she spoke to the whole class. "I hope you all realize that *no* one can go on the field trip unless I have a permission slip signed by one of your parents. If you come to school tomorrow without your slip, you'll just have to sit in the library and do worksheets all day. No excuses —this is your responsibility! Ah-choo, ah-choo, ah-choo!" She blew her nose. "For fifth graders, you certainly don't always accept responsibility the way you should."

Maureen thought how much crabbier Miss Welgloss had gotten since the spring pollen season started. Actually she was a pretty nice teacher, when her allergies weren't bothering her. Maureen motioned to Kitty to follow her back to their seats—and saw with surprise that Kitty was about to say something to the teacher.

"Speaking of responsibility, Miss Welgloss, that reminds me of the funniest thing that Maureen did when she was about three." Smoothing her hair back, Kitty smiled to herself. "She was walking sort of uncomfortably, you know, and looking unhappy, so I asked her what the matter was. And she said"—Kitty laughed an indulgent little laugh—"she said, 'Somebody wet my pants.' She was so cute!"

Maureen stood paralyzed as the last dreadful words

came out of Kitty's mouth. A wave of heat flowed upward through her face, and then her hands felt cold. For a brief moment, she hoped that no one else had heard. But then the shouts of laughter broke out behind her.

Miss Welgloss looked surprised and embarrassed, herself. Giving Kitty an uneasy smile, she turned back to the class. "Quiet! *Medley* readers, it's time for you to go to Mr. Starr's room."

Grabbing Kitty's elbow, Maureen trudged grimly to her desk. She didn't look at anyone, but she heard Gwen drawl, "*Isn't* she cute?" Maureen would never live this down, never, never. Plopping into her seat, she shoved a reader at Kitty. "Just read this. And don't say anything else!"

Kitty's face looked hurt and bewildered, but Maureen didn't care. No one would ever forget that awful story! Never, never! If there was any chance of forgetting, Gwen would remind them. For the rest of her life, Maureen would be the girl who said, "Somebody wet my pants."

Glancing sideways at Kitty, Maureen wished for the first time that she had never asked Mr. Costue for a new friend. Kitty had been nothing but trouble—and now this! How *could* she tell that awful story on Maureen? Mom herself wouldn't have done that, even though she was a grown-up. It seemed that Kitty had the worst parts of Mom's personality, but not her good sense.

Maureen wished she could just walk out of the classroom and go home and call Mr. Costue right now. She felt tired—almost old, as if she were a mother herself, trying to manage a difficult child. But somehow she would have to suffer through the rest of the morning and lunch and the afternoon, until dismissal time.

Kitty was leaning over to whisper to her. "You shouldn't be so touchy. Can't you take a joke on yourself?" When Maureen didn't answer, she went on, "But never mind; I'm not angry with you."

"Wonderful," muttered Maureen.

At lunchtime, Maureen took Kitty to the girls' rest room and stayed there for a long time, until she thought everyone else must be in the lunchroom, eating. Then she and Kitty could sit at a table far away from the rest of Maureen's class.

But when they reached the spaghetti-smelling lunchroom, there was no extra space at any of the tables—except the table where Tracey's dark head and Gwen's light head showed plainly. "There," said Kitty brightly, motioning with her tray. "There are two seats over there."

Glumly Maureen edged in next to Jody, while Kitty sat down opposite, next to Tracey. Gwen was on the other side of Tracey, and Amanda on the other side of Jody. The next table was filled with the boys from Miss Welgloss's class, including Marvin. Maureen felt their stares and heard their laughter, although she pretended not to.

For a moment, Maureen hoped that Gwen would leave her alone for now. She took a bite of spaghetti, keeping her eyes on her plate.

"Did you get to the girls' room in time?" Gwen's voice, full of mock concern, dashed her hope. "Or did *somebody*—you know what?"

Raising her eyes for a moment, Maureen saw Tracey give a shrug and a little smile. No help from her ex-best friend. And Kitty, sitting next to Tracey, wasn't paying attention. She was gazing down at her spaghetti, chewing very slowly, as if she thought it tasted awful.

"I've got a good idea," Gwen went on. "Why don't you bring an extra pair of pants to school, just in case?"

Maureen wondered how many weeks she would have to stay in from recess if she threw her plate of spaghetti in Gwen's face.

"Oh, shut up, Gwen."

Maureen turned with surprise to see Jody frowning at Gwen. And Amanda wasn't smiling, either.

"A joke isn't a joke anymore, the tenth time around," Jody went on.

But Gwen couldn't be shut up so easily. "Gee, I wasn't joking. I just wanted to make sure Maureen wasn't—"

"Alien clone!"

All the girls looked up at Marvin, who had paused on his way to the counter. He was pointing his empty tray straight at Gwen, his eyes rolling. "An alien

clone!" he exclaimed again, turning to the boys' table. "You can tell them by their green hair!"

The girls turned to stare at Gwen. Her rough blonde hair did look sort of greenish, Maureen realized. Had she never noticed it before, or was it the light?

Jody smothered a giggle. Maureen felt her spirits rise.

But Gwen eyed Marvin from under half-closed lids. "That's just from swim team, you twerp. The chlorine in the water does it. Little monkeys don't know much about sports, do they?"

"Alien clone! Alien clone!" chanted Marvin. The other boys were jumping up, surrounding the girls' table, pointing at Gwen. "Alien clone! Alien clone!"

Abruptly Gwen stood up, bumping into the boy behind her. "Come on, Tracey."

As the two girls left, the lunch aide hurried over to make the boys quiet down and shoo them out to recess. Maureen looked happily around the girls' table, realizing they were glad Gwen had been embarrassed. Amanda sang, "It's not easy, being green. . . ." The girls sputtered with laughter.

Kitty looked amused, but puzzled. "He's a funny kid, isn't he?" she asked, gazing after Marvin. " 'Alien clone!' Where did he ever get that idea?"

Maureen began to eat her spaghetti with a better appetite. Maybe she wouldn't call Mr. Costue this afternoon, after all. Jody and Amanda, anyway, didn't seem to hold it against Maureen that her new friend was a little weird. And if Marvin could take on Gwen like that—! Maureen felt the highest regard for Marvin. He wasn't just a funny kid. He was a *good* kid—even if he did look something like Curious George.

"How am I going to get to my ballet lesson?" demanded Alison. She was standing in front of the garage in her blue leotard and tights, hands on hips, blocking Maureen from wheeling her bike out. "Mommy forgot about my ballet lesson!"

Maureen had certainly forgotten that Alison went to ballet class on Thursdays. What a pain! Now Maureen would have to produce more explanations. "Mom didn't forget, but she couldn't help it. She said you'd just have to skip ballet this week."

"I can't skip it!" Alison looked as if she might burst into tears. "Mrs. Hopper said we had to come to every rehearsal or we couldn't be in the recital."

"Well, I can't drive you there," said Maureen. "Why don't you ride your bike?"

"On Main Street? Mommy doesn't let me ride on Main Street—there's too much traffic." But even as she spoke, Alison was squeezing between Maureen and the station wagon to get her bike. "Oh, well, this is different."

"It's just this once," agreed Maureen.

But Kitty, who had been watching from the stone wall, slid to the ground. Her face was drawn with alarm. "Oh, no, Alison. I don't think you should ride your bike to ballet. I'm sure your teacher will understand why you couldn't come today. . . . I'll call her and explain."

"No!" blurted Maureen. Alison, wheeling her bike out of the garage, just gave Kitty a puzzled look.

"Alison," Kitty tried again, "why don't you walk to your lesson? I'll come along with you."

"I don't have time." Alison swung herself onto her bike. "Why are you worried, Kitty? I'll be fine."

Maureen was getting worried herself—worried that Alison and Kitty would get into a discussion of why Kitty was so concerned about Alison. "No, Alison doesn't have time," she said loudly. "In fact, Alison, you'd better hurry if you're going to get there on time even with your bike."

As Alison pedaled off down the driveway, her light hair floating out behind, Kitty took a few steps after her. "Ride facing the traffic!" she called. "Walk your bike across intersections!"

Maureen felt a twinge of guilt. Was it really all right to let Alison ride her clunky little-kid's bike all the way down Main Street to her ballet class? But Alison knew the safety rules. Besides, Maureen had ridden her bike on Main Street at Alison's age. For some reason Mom was more cautious with Alison.

Pushing her own bike out of the garage, Maureen handed it to Kitty. "Here, you can ride my bike, and I'll ride Mom's." It seemed like an odd arrangement, but Kitty wouldn't have been comfortable on Mom's bike. It was too big for her.

Kitty was still gazing worriedly in the direction Alison had taken. "I hope she remembers to give hand signals."

"She'll be fine." Impatiently Maureen swung her leg over her mother's bicycle. The words *You're not her mother* were on the tip of her tongue, but she swallowed them and hitched up the shoulder straps of her backpack. "Let's go."

Gliding down the S curves of Chestnut Hill Road, Maureen patted her pants pocket, which held the money from her mother's purse. She had felt uneasy, taking money from Mom's wallet without asking. But it wasn't stealing, she reminded herself, because she was just buying groceries—as her mother would have done if she were here. Only she *was* here, sort of. . . . Never mind!

Maureen liked riding her mother's bike, which wheeled along more smoothly and easily than her own. Maureen had expected the seat to be too high for her, so that she would have to stand up all the way to the A&P, but actually she only had to stretch her legs a little to pedal.

Braking at the stop sign at the corner of Cooper Street, Maureen glanced over her shoulder to make sure Kitty was right behind her. Kitty was, smoothing a wisp of hair back toward her pony tail, with that look on her face as if she didn't quite know what was going on.

Well, that wasn't surprising. Maureen sighed, pedaling down Cooper Street to Main Street. She was responsible for Kitty. She was also responsible for Alison, since Mom wasn't here. She was the one who had to see that Alison got to her ballet lesson; she was the one who had to plan dinner. Let's see, she could cook hamburgers without any problem. . . .

It was a perfect day, the blue sky washed clear by yesterday's rain. Pumping past a lilac hedge, Maureen sniffed the blossoms' perfume, but she couldn't spend much time enjoying the balmy afternoon. Maureen had to plan, because she was in charge.

9

Cold Turkey

By the time Maureen and Kitty were parking their bikes by the gumball machine outside the A&P, Kitty's mind seemed to have cleared. "What should we get for dinner?" she asked briskly, watching Maureen lock their bikes together. "Something good, to take the taste of that school spaghetti out of our mouths. Let's see, we'll need some kind of meat, and a green or yellow vegetable—maybe spinach or squash—"

Maureen glanced up in dismay. "I don't know how to cook all that stuff. I was thinking of hamburgers. Anyway, one thing we *have* to get is something for sandwiches for the field trip tomorrow. . . ." Maureen's voice trailed off as she stared past Kitty at the pink van parked in front of the Costue and Fader office. Something had caught her eye as she rode past the back of the van. What was it?

"What are you looking at?" asked Kitty.

Giving the combination lock a twist, Maureen straightened up and walked around to the back of the van. Yes. It was the license plate. It was not the same one she had noticed yesterday afternoon. Yesterday the license plate of the van had read FRIEND.

But today the pink van's license plate said CONQER. *Conquer*, without the *u*.

"Well, what is it?" asked Kitty.

Maureen shook her head to clear it. Maybe she was wrong. Maybe the license plate of the Costue and Fader van had been CONQER all along. So much had happened in the last two days, it was hard to remember. Anyway, so what if they had changed the license plate? What would that mean?

"Nothing, I guess," she said to herself and Kitty. She turned back toward the A&P.

Inside the store, Kitty skillfully jerked a cart from a jammed-together row and started down the frozen foods aisle. "Leaf spinach . . . and mashed butternut squash . . ."

"We don't need *two* vegetables." Maureen tried without success to ease the shopping cart away from Kitty. "If we get a lot of other stuff, we might not have enough money for ice cream."

Kitty didn't seem to hear. She was pointing at a bin

of frozen turkeys. "That's what we should have for dinner—turkey. Then we could have turkey sandwiches for lunch tomorrow. Don't you love roast turkey, with dressing and cranberry sauce?"

Maureen looked doubtfully at the lumpy birds. "But I don't know how to cook turkeys."

"Roasting a turkey is easy." Kitty waved a hand carelessly. "You just put the stuffing in"—she plucked a box of stuffing from the shelf above the turkeys—"and stick the turkey in the oven, and then take it out when it's done. There's just one little thing you have to remember. It slips my mind right now, but I'm sure it'll come to me when we get home."

"How—" Maureen shut her mouth. She had been about to ask Kitty how she knew about roasting turkeys. "Okay." Leaning over the freezer bin, Maureen picked up one of the smaller turkeys. It was heavy, and so cold it hurt her hands. But there were instructions right on the plastic casing: To Thaw and To Cook. So it couldn't be that difficult.

Outside the A&P once more, Kitty eased her grocery bag into the basket on Maureen's bike. "It's a good thing we didn't buy any more groceries. This just fits."

"I know, I'll have to carry this," said Maureen, wiggling her backpack over the frozen turkey. She was staring at the girl marching up to the door of the Costue and Fader office.

It was Jody. Under her thick bangs her eyes looked

101

anxious, and she clutched a piece of pink paper in one hand. She didn't turn to look at Maureen and Kitty.

Maureen felt an impulse to run after her and tell her not to turn in the Friend Loss Report. Jody needing friend insurance? That was ridiculous. Even if something was wrong between her and Amanda, Maureen was sure there were other girls in their class who would want to be friends with Jody.

But if Maureen tried to talk Jody out of giving Mr. Costue the report, what would she say? After all, Maureen had done the same thing, and she had gotten what she asked for . . . more or less. Also, Maureen felt she would rather not have to explain to anyone exactly how friend insurance worked. Not until after the field trip, anyway.

With an exasperated shrug Maureen jumped onto her bike and coasted across the sloping parking lot, followed by Kitty. After all, she couldn't be responsible for Jody, too!

Then the bike jounced over a rut in the asphalt, and the turkey thumped Maureen's back. She almost lost her balance, but the jolt took her mind off her responsibilities. Gripping the handlebars, she steered toward the exit.

It was awkward and uncomfortable, riding her bike with a cold, heavy turkey on her back, but Maureen made it home without falling off. In the kitchen she swung the backpack from her shoulders and onto the counter with a *clunk*.

Setting the grocery bag on the kitchen table, Kitty looked over with a start. "Was that the turkey?" She reached out and poked it through the backpack. "It's frozen pretty solid."

"You should try riding a bike with it," said Maureen. "My back is black-and-blue." Wiggling the turkey out of the backpack, she leaned over to read the directions on its stony breast.

"Keep frozen until ready to roast and serve," the directions began. There was certainly no problem there. "Use cold running water"—that must mean in the kitchen sink—"2 to 6 hours for fastest thaw, or—"

Kitty, reading over Maureen's shoulder, gasped. "Oh, no! That was it!"

"That was *what*?"

"That was the one little thing I was trying to remember about frozen turkeys." Kitty's voice trailed off. "They take a long time to defrost."

Maureen looked at the clock on the stove. It was almost four thirty now. Even if the turkey thawed in only two hours, it would be six thirty, the Harritys' usual dinnertime, before they could put it in the oven.

"Maybe it won't take that long to roast," suggested Maureen. "It's a small turkey." She bent over the directions again, reading the chart telling how long to cook different weights of turkeys. The smallest was "12 lbs —4 hrs."

"*Four hours!*" exclaimed Maureen and Kitty together. Kitty went on unhappily. "We won't be able to eat dinner until . . . ten thirty."

Maureen gave Kitty a look. " 'Roasting a turkey is easy.' Great idea, Kitty."

"Well, it *is* easy." Kitty nervously smoothed her hair back with both hands. "It just takes longer than I . . ."

Gazing at the naked frozen turkey, Maureen thought of the turkey drumstick with crackly brown skin that she had been looking forward to. She thought about the peanut butter and bread, with squash and spinach, that they would have to eat for dinner. "Yeah," she said. "Just one little problem." She shoved the turkey into the sink with a bang, making the cupboard doors rattle. "I guess we'd better get started."

Maureen turned on the cold water, thinking grumpily about staying up until ten thirty to take the turkey out of the oven. She felt tired already. Why had she counted on Kitty to know what she was talking about? Sometimes Kitty acted as if she knew everything Mom would know, but other times it was plain that the inside of her head was pretty mixed up. Maureen had to remember that she, Maureen, was in charge while Kitty was here, and she shouldn't expect any help from Kitty.

The jingling of the telephone broke into Maureen's thoughts. Kitty, who had been standing awkwardly near the sink, went to answer the phone.

Pushing the turkey around under the stream of water, Maureen waited for Kitty to say, "It's for you" or "for Alison" or "for your mother." But what she actually heard Kitty say was, "Alison? Very funny, Frank." Her tone was jokingly affectionate.

Frank! Staring at Kitty, Maureen suddenly felt as cold as the turkey. It must be Dad, calling from Montreal. What would he think of a girl talking to him like his wife? Frantically she dried her hands on a towel.

"All right, that's enough." Now Kitty sounded annoyed. "When is your flight coming in Saturday?" Then a dazed expression came over her face. She held the phone away from her ear, squinting at it as if she wondered how she happened to be holding it.

Maureen grabbed the phone from Kitty. "Hi, Dad."

Her father laughed in a mystified way. "Maureen, what's going on? Is Alison pulling my leg?"

"No, that was my friend Kitty." Maureen shot a look at Kitty, who was now standing at the sink, gazing down at the turkey as if it were a crystal ball that could solve a mystery for her. "She does sound a lot like Alison, doesn't she? Well, anyway, how's the convention?"

"Boring, honey. There's no action here, so I'm leaving a day early. I have to talk to Mom about picking me up at the airport. Is she there?"

"Picking you up at the airport—*tomorrow*?" Maureen imagined Kitty sitting beside her on the field trip bus while Dad waited at the airport. She stiffened with panic. "Oh—I don't think she can."

"Of course she can." Dad sounded annoyed. "In fact, it's very convenient for her, because she'll be in Boston anyway for her biology class, and—" He stopped short. "This is silly. Let me talk to your mother."

Maureen clutched at the receiver as it slipped in her damp hand. "Er—she isn't here right now. May I take a message?"

Her father's disbelieving laugh rang through the wires. " 'May I take a message?' Come on, Maureen. You sound like you're practicing for finishing school. This is Dad you're talking to, remember?" He paused. "Is something going on? Has there been a palace revolution while I was gone—do you have your mother tied up and gagged in the basement?"

Maureen's stomach flipped, but she forced a laugh. Of course he was just kidding. "Sorry, Dad," she said in a strained voice. "Do you want Mom to call you back?" She wrote down the number he gave her and hung up.

Kitty, still at the sink, was trying to pinch the turkey. "It doesn't seem to be getting any softer."

"Maybe it would thaw faster if we took the bag off," said Maureen. Pulling a knife from the knife rack, she sawed at the bunched end of the bag. What was she going to do about Dad? If Mom didn't call him back this evening, he would call again. Could Maureen pretend that Mom had left a message for him that he would have to get home from the airport by himself? But Maureen didn't want him to come home tomorrow at all—she wanted him to stay away until Saturday. How could she persuade him to do that?

A drop of sweat trickled down the side of her face as Maureen tugged the plastic bag off of the turkey. Her hair was hanging over her cheeks, making her hotter, but she couldn't brush it back with her messy hands. "I'm going to turn on the hot water, too. The cold isn't doing any good."

"I'm not sure you're supposed to use hot water," said Kitty. She picked up the plastic bag to look at the directions again. "Oh, no! Maureen, it says, 'Do not remove bag to thaw.' "

Maureen groaned. She turned off the water, and the two of them struggled to fit the cold, slippery turkey back into the plastic bag. But it wouldn't go back in, any more than Maureen could have wiggled into last summer's shorts.

"You should have finished reading the directions before you took the bag off," said Kitty.

Maureen stared at her in disbelief. "*I* should have read the directions? It's *my* fault we're stuck with this stupid turkey?" Forgetting about being in charge and mature and responsible, Maureen let words burst out of her mouth. "I'm getting pretty tired of your advice, Kitty. Why don't you just go—just go read the paper and leave me alone?"

Kitty drew back. For a moment, seeing her deep-set eyes flash, Maureen was afraid Kitty was going to punish her for talking that way to her mother. But then Kitty looked away from Maureen, sighing. "All right," she said in a distant tone. "If you're going to take that attitude, I will go read the paper."

As Kitty stalked off to the family room, Maureen stared glumly at the turkey. It wasn't Kitty's fault, even though she *was* irritating. Whose fault was it? Mr. Costue's? He was the one who had given her the friend insurance, who had seemed so sure that Kitty would be the perfect friend for Maureen. But Mr. Costue, Maureen admitted to herself, was completely mistaken about that. Even though he and Mr. Fader had gone to a lot of trouble, using up-to-date ideas and molecular biology and computers and so on, it just wasn't a very good idea to try to make a best friend out of someone's mother.

Hearing the kitchen door open, Maureen turned to see Alison in her blue leotard twirling into the kitchen. "La, la-la, la, la. I'm going to ask Mommy if I can ride my bike to ballet from now on." Pointing her toes with each step, she pranced to the sink and leaned over the pinkish gray, lumpy bird. "Ugh. Is that raw chicken?"

"It's going to be roast turkey, dummy." Maureen turned it under the hot water. "I just have to thaw it first." She didn't want to talk about the turkey. "Oh, by the way, Dad called."

"Is he coming home?" asked Alison hopefully.

"Tomorrow. He wanted Mom to pick him up at the airport."

"But she's in New Hampshire."

"Yeah. . . ." Maureen had gotten on the wrong subject again. "Maybe she'll drive down to Boston tomorrow and pick Dad up. I don't know." She paused, then thought of something else. "I told him to call her at Aunt Marcia's—maybe they don't need her there anymore." Glancing up from the turkey, Maureen noticed Alison staring blankly at the counter, as if she was remembering something disturbing. "What's the matter?"

But Alison didn't answer. Whirling, she ran to the basement door. Maureen heard her ballet shoes pattering down the stairs. What had gotten into her?

Maureen turned the turkey again. The skin felt softer now, but Maureen could tell that just underneath it was still rock-hard. Balancing the turkey on its tail, she let the hot water run inside. She was beginning to hate the turkey. What if she just stuck it in the oven and hoped for the best? She hoisted it onto the counter, wondering what pan to cook it in.

Then the sound of feet pounding up the basement stairs distracted Maureen from the turkey. As she glanced over her shoulder, Alison burst through the door, her mouth working and her eyes staring. In her blue leotard and tights she looked like a distressed elf, a funny sight if she weren't screaming at Maureen.

"Where's Mommy?"

Maureen was shaken, but she tried to answer in a calm voice. "I told you, she's helping Aunt—"

"No, she isn't! You made that all up, you liar, Maureen! You must think I'm really stupid. Mommy didn't drive to New Hampshire, and she can't drive down to Boston, either, because her car's in the garage! And so is Daddy's!" She stepped closer, the cords in her neck standing out. *"Where's Mommy?"*

"A little quieter in there, please," came Kitty's voice from the family room.

Holding on to the turkey's drumsticks as if she could steer her way out of this mess, Maureen took a deep breath. If Kitty came into the kitchen now, and Alison realized—! "Alison, calm down." She tried to smile reassuringly. "I—er—just made a mistake when I said she drove. She took a bus—I forgot." But she could see that Alison didn't believe a word.

"All right," said Alison grimly. "I'm going to call Mommy at Aunt Marcia's." She opened the drawer near the telephone and took out the address book.

"No!" Maureen steadied the slippery turkey on the edge of the counter and wiped her hands. "She—she said we shouldn't call her unless it was an emergency. . . . Alison, you'd better not do that."

Paying no attention, Alison opened the book and began to dial.

If Alison talked to Aunt Marcia, Maureen would be in real trouble! There would be no chance of her straightening everything out by herself. Maureen sprang at her little sister, seizing her arm.

But with surprising strength Alison shoved Maureen away, sending her reeling back along the counter. Maureen felt her elbow brush something, and in an instant that seemed to last an hour she saw the turkey topple on the edge of the counter. Struggling to get her balance back, she clutched at the turkey, but it slipped through her hands . . . and fell like a boulder from a cliff onto Maureen's sneaker-clad foot.

"Oww!" The room blurred before Maureen's eyes. Grabbing for the kitchen counter, she missed . . . and found herself sitting on the floor next to the turkey.

Alison was staring down at her sister, her hand to her mouth. "I'm sorry." Her voice was muffled. "I didn't mean to. Does it hurt?"

Did it hurt. Maureen gasped, feeling the waves of pain wash up her leg through her knee and thigh. She gritted her teeth so that she wouldn't cry in front of her little sister—and then realized that tears were already running down her cheeks.

"Maureen!" Kitty was standing in the door to the family room, still holding the newspaper. "You've *hurt* yourself—and there's no adult at home. This is just the kind of thing I was afraid would happen."

"Want me to get the Band-Aids?" Alison hovered over Maureen. "Should I call Mrs. Argos?"

"*No.*" Maureen tried to ignore the pangs pulsing up

her leg. One thing was very clear: She had to get hold of Mr. Costue, right now. She had to let Kitty go this afternoon; there was no way around it. Alison couldn't be fooled any longer, and very soon Dad was going to find out Mom was missing. And . . . Maureen was sick and tired of being in charge. She wanted her mother back.

10

The Wonderful Plan

Holding on to the counter, Maureen hauled herself up. She could put some weight on her left foot if she let only the heel touch the floor. Still leaning on the counter, she started to hitch herself over to the phone. Then she hesitated, looking first at Alison and then at Kitty. She didn't want to talk to Mr. Costue in front of them. Should she go into her parents' bedroom and call? No. She couldn't trust Alison not to listen on the kitchen phone.

Maureen would have to ride her bike to the Costue and Fader office.

Oh, no. Maureen bit her lip to keep from groaning. Ride all the way to the A&P and back again, this time with her foot hurting?

But Maureen didn't see any other choice. Anyway,

it would be better to talk to Mr. Costue in person. Besides telling him to change Kitty back, Maureen really wanted to make him understand that friend insurance was not a good idea, before he tried it on Jody or anyone else.

"All right," said Maureen to Alison. "I know where Mom is, but I have to go get her. It's not too far."

"I'll come, too," said Alison.

"No! I mean—that won't work." Putting her head down, Maureen took a deep breath. "You and Kitty have to stay here. I can't tell you why, but if you come with me, we won't be able to get Mom."

"Somebody kidnapped her," whispered Alison. She stared pale-faced at Maureen. "What if they kidnap you, too?"

Maureen shook her head. It was so hard to explain without really explaining! "It's not like that. It's a secret, but not a bad secret. But you and Kitty have to stay here, all right?" She thought of the black transformer on the power lines. "I mean, *in* the house until I come back. That's very important!"

While Alison and Maureen were talking, Kitty stood looking from one to the other with a strained expression, as if they were speaking in a foreign language that she had once known. Now she put her hands to her head. "I need some aspirin. And a cup of coffee."

"You help Kitty, Alison, okay? Please!" Maureen hobbled toward the door. "I'll be back soon."

At least the way to the A&P was mostly downhill, thought Maureen as she wheeled her bike out of the garage again. She wouldn't have to pump much at all. Mounting awkwardly, she pedaled down the driveway in a limping fashion.

As she coasted downhill, Maureen tried to keep her mind off her throbbing foot by rehearsing what she would say to Mr. Costue. This time she mustn't let him talk her out of changing her mother back—she had to make him understand that Kitty wasn't satisfactory. "It isn't really like having a friend," she said to him in her mind. "It's like *I'm* the mother, and I have to take care of everything." And then there was the matter of Jody and the other girls. Without hurting his feelings, Maureen had to explain to Mr. Costue that it wouldn't be helpful to turn their mothers into friends, either. "Friend insurance was a great idea, Mr. Costue," she would say tactfully, "but I'm afraid it isn't working out."

Maureen came out of her thoughts on Main Street, suddenly aware that someone else was riding a bicycle only half a block ahead of her. Frowning, she focused her gaze, and saw that it was Marvin Smith. He was hunched over his handlebars, his elbows out and his legs pumping nimbly.

Maureen might be glad to see Marvin some other time, but she didn't want to run into him right now. The A&P was just ahead, and she didn't want Marvin to see her going into the Costue and Fader office, or to ask her any questions. Probably Marvin was going to the A&P for his mother. Maureen slowed down a little to give him time to get into the store.

But to her dismay Marvin parked his bike next to the Costue and Fader office. Flattening himself against the wall, he cautiously peered in the window of the office, then quickly drew back. What did he think he was doing?

Trying to appear unconcerned, Maureen leaned her bike against the wall. "Hi, Marvin." She started to pull open the office door.

"Sh!" Marvin shrank farther back from the window, glaring at her. "I don't want to let them know they're being watched." Then his expression turned to alarm. "You aren't going in there, are you?"

Marvin and his silly science fiction plot! He might ruin everything. "Marvin, this is not a game," she said in a dignified tone. "It's a serious matter involving my mother. So—"

"I knew it." Marvin stared at her sternly. "They're making clones of mothers. That's why I came here— to get proof before I went to the police."

Maureen's heart sank. She had ridden all this way, with pains jabbing up from her foot, so that no one would know she was talking to Mr. Costue. And now here was Marvin! If he stirred up a big mess with the police, it might be quite a while before she got her mother back.

Then she had an inspiration—she would pretend to

go along with him. "This is amazing!" she whispered. "That's why I'm here, too. We can cooperate. I'll go into the office to look for evidence because Mr. Costue knows me and won't suspect me. *You* stay outside in case I need help."

Marvin looked as if he would have liked it the other way around, but he nodded reluctantly. "Okay." He pulled a pocket magnifying glass from his jeans and knelt down on the sidewalk. "I'll just pretend I'm watching ants here."

Maureen wished Marvin could have come up with a more likely excuse to be lurking outside the Costue and Fader office. However, this was no time to argue. Pulling open the door, she limped in.

Mr. Costue was not at his desk in front of the divider, but the lights were on in the back of the office. Through the palm fronds and ferns and spider plants Maureen could see the top of Mr. Fader's dark head bent over the computer terminal hood. Maybe Mr. Costue was back there, too. "Hello?" she called.

Mr. Fader's droopy face popped up. "The office is closed," he called. "Come back tomorrow at nine o'-clock." He sank out of sight again.

Maureen sighed. She didn't want to talk to Mr. Fader—he seemed so peculiar. But she couldn't leave, either. She hobbled around the divider to the back of the room, where the computer terminal perched on top of a row of metal cabinets. Maureen noticed thick cables arching from each end of the row to outlets in the floor, like a spider's legs.

Leaning over the cabinets, Maureen cleared her throat. "Mr. Fader, I have to talk to you about something very important."

Mr. Fader looked as though he wanted to crawl into a cabinet. His eyes flickering away from Maureen and back again, he hunched up his sagging shoulders. "No —no. I—I don't talk to people. I'm just the molecular biologist. Mr. Costue handles interpersonal communications, but he isn't here." He brushed his lank hair out of his eyes. "Please go away."

"I didn't really mean that you had to talk," said Maureen wearily. "I just want you to change my mother back. Remember, I called yesterday about my mother, Mrs. Harrity? She's supposed to be thirty-eight."

Peering over Maureen's shoulder, Mr. Fader cracked his knuckles. "Yes, I remember," he said. "After that, Will and I agreed that I shouldn't try to talk to anyone, because I might give people the wrong impression about our business. So if you want to talk to someone, go sit down"—he motioned to the front of the office—"and wait for Mr. Costue. He's out with the van, installing transformers, but he'll be back in a minute."

Installing transformers! Maureen definitely had to talk to Mr. Costue. Meanwhile, she *would* like to sit down, to take the weight from her aching foot. She started for the front of the office, then hesitated. "But why can't you change my mother back now? Mr. Costue said you had her DNA code and you could do it any time."

Mr. Fader looked distressed. "Did Will tell you that? I guess he thought you would be upset if he—well, actually it wasn't a lie. We do have the code in the data bank. Will wouldn't lie to anyone unless he had to." Again he brushed back the strands of hair falling over his forehead.

Maureen felt dizzy, as if the floor had tipped under her feet. "What do you mean? Do you mean . . . Do you mean you can turn my mother back, but you *won't*?"

Fiddling with his baggy tie, Mr. Fader rolled his eyes around the room. "It's so hard to explain. If you'll just wait until Will comes back . . . he's good at explaining."

"But just tell me!" Fear choked Maureen's voice. "Why won't you turn Kitty back into my mother?"

Mr. Fader sighed, gazing hopelessly over the palm fronds, toward the door. "I don't know what's taking Will so long. Well . . . you see, William Costue has a wonderful plan for saving our country. I suppose you know we're in a terrible state? Unemployment, inflation, injustice, divorces, tasteless tomatoes?"

"I guess so," said Maureen. Now that she thought of it, she had heard her parents talking in serious tones about some of those things. "But I don't—"

"Well—Will is going to fix all that." A proud smile pulled up Mr. Fader's sagging face.

Maureen laughed, mystified. "But he can't fix all that! No one can."

"Oh, yes." Mr. Fader nodded eagerly, leaning toward her over the computer terminal hood. "Because it's due to a surplus of adults."

Maureen stopped laughing. "It is?" she whispered. She was beginning to have an inkling of what he was getting at. A cold spot of fear in her stomach spread out into the rest of her body, and she shivered.

"Yes, don't you see?" Mr. Fader spread his hands. "Will went right to the heart of the problem. What insight! There are just too many adults running everything now—that's why the country is such a mess. 'Too many cooks spoil the broth,' says Will. So he thought, if only most of the adults could be turned into children—" He gazed hopefully at Maureen. "Did I explain it right? Do you understand?"

Maureen felt herself shaking all over. She could barely speak. "But if the grown-ups weren't running the country—who would run it?" And then, in the instant before Mr. Fader spoke, she knew the answer.

"William Costue," said Mr. Fader happily. "He has so many good ideas already. And he's great at dealing with people—a genius, don't you think?" His voice sank reverently, as if he were in church. "And I have the great happiness and honor to be chosen for his partner, to sort the biological data and operate the central computer."

"Mr. Costue." Maureen clutched the top of the cabinets, afraid that her legs might crumple. Friendly Mr. Costue, who only wanted to help people.

"Will likes me to call him William the Conqueror, sometimes," said Mr. Fader fondly. "It's our joke. Maybe you noticed the new license plate I got for the van? Will has a great sense of humor, doesn't he?"

Maureen stared at him, speechless. All the grown-ups, including Mom and Dad and Miss Welgloss, turned backward into boys and girls? And Mr. Costue and Mr. Fader, the only grown-ups left, running the country! Marvin had been right—not about alien clones, maybe, but right that there was a plot.

And she, Maureen, had been helping them with the plot. She had handed out all those leaflets. She had given them Mom's hair, from which they had gotten her DNA information to put into the computer. And —Maureen drew in her breath sharply—she had given them Dad's hair, too!

"Then you're going to turn my father into a boy!" she exclaimed.

"As soon as he comes into your house, within reach of the transformer," agreed Mr. Fader. "And then you'll have two new friends, instead of just one." He spread his hands again. "Will wants everyone to have friends and be happy. People are so unhappy nowadays! I was unhappy, too, before Will found me in a supermarket one day, buying cases of lemon gelatin. Will wants everyone to be friends, the way he and I are friends."

"So he can run the country," said Maureen in a faint voice. Her mind darted this way and that. She glanced toward the front of the store, hoping that Marvin might be peering in the window again. If only she could signal him to run for the police!

No, no. If the police came, why would they believe Maureen's story? Mr. Fader certainly wouldn't be so stupid as to tell *them* what he and Mr. Costue were up to. And even if they did believe Maureen and took Mr. Fader and Mr. Costue away in handcuffs, who would be able to change her mother back?

"That's right, so he can run the country the way it ought to be run," said Mr. Fader in a pleased tone. "We're getting everything ready. Will had a new flag made—it just came today. Would you like to see it?" Reaching a flat cardboard box down from the top of a filing cabinet, he shook out a silky rectangle, as big as the United States flag in Miss Welgloss's classroom, and held it up for Maureen to see. "What do you think?"

Maureen stared at it numbly. On a pink background, a white circle enclosed the double twisted ribbons. The DNA molecule. "That's going to be the new flag of the United States?" she whispered.

"We're going to call it the United Friends of America," said Mr. Fader. "And after everything's squared away here, there are other countries that need help, too. Will can tell you more about it when he gets back. What could be taking him so long, I wonder?"

Maureen had to do something, and do it fast.

"Don't you like our flag?" asked Mr. Fader.

Maureen looked at his face, eager and droopy like a basset hound's. "Yes," she said slowly. "I think it's— very nice." Mr. Fader didn't seem like a bad man—just sort of silly. If he had been talked into the plan by Mr. Costue, maybe he could be talked out of it, at least as far as Maureen's mother was concerned.

But what could she say that would make Mr. Fader disobey his partner?

A flash of an idea lit up Maureen's mind, and her heart pounded against her ribs. "Er—Mr. Fader, I guess it'll be pretty wonderful when you and Mr. Costue are the only two grown-ups left, and you're running the world together."

Mr. Fader's sagging face lifted, pleased that she understood him. "Yes. Won't it be great? Will and me. And we'll make everyone so happy."

Folding her arms, Maureen spoke in a hard voice. "But what makes you think Mr. Costue isn't going to turn *you* into a kid, too?"

"What?" The smile drained from Mr. Fader's face.

"Why should he let you run things with him?" she

asked deliberately. "He's probably planning to turn you into a three-year-old as soon as he has the world under control."

"Stop that!" Mr. Fader's droopy lips were trembling. "Don't talk that way about Will! He's my best friend. He couldn't get along without me. He told me so."

"Yeah," said Maureen. "And he 'wouldn't lie to anyone unless he had to.'" She could see she was getting to Mr. Fader. "I bet he's just being nice to you, so you'll do the biology work for his plan. And when it's all done, I bet he's planning to turn you into a kid."

Folding up the pink flag with fumbling fingers, Mr. Fader stuffed it into the cardboard box and threw it back on top of the filing cabinet. "No!" he muttered to himself. "Will is my true-blue friend, forever and ever." He began to walk back and forth in front of the computer terminal, running his fingers through his limp hair.

Then Mr. Fader stopped short, turning on Maureen with a triumphant snort. "And I can prove it!"

"How could you prove it?" Maureen held her breath.

"Very simply," snapped Mr. Fader. He motioned toward the computer terminal. "First I'd give the instruction 'Prepare to transform.' Then I'd supply my name, Horace Bindle Fader. Then, since my DNA code *isn't* in the data bank, the screen would display 'Transformation not possible—insufficient information.' " He laughed scornfully. "Whereas if Will *had* plugged my DNA code into the computer, the screen would show, 'Ready to transform.' "

"Go ahead, then," said Maureen. "Prove it." She shoved her trembling hands into her pockets. She had just said that about Mr. Costue to arouse Mr. Fader's suspicions. *Would* he have put Mr. Fader's DNA information into the data bank, ready to transform? If only he had!

Mr. Fader scowled at her. "Well . . ." He made a motion toward the computer terminal. Then his face brightened as he gazed over Maureen's shoulder. "Never mind. There's Will now. He'll explain everything."

11

A Friend in Need

Her heart plummeting, Maureen stood on tiptoe to see, over the divider, the pink van pulling up in front of the office. Mr. Costue swung out of the driver's seat and strolled in the door, whistling "High Hopes." His face shone pinker than ever through the palm fronds.

"Twelve transformers installed today with no problems, Horace," he called. "They all thought I was from the power company." He tossed a round black transformer into the air, catching it neatly. "And I *am*! Costue and Fader, power unlimited! Let's transform the mother of that girl who turned in her Friend Loss Report this afternoon, right now." Then his eye fell on Maureen. He stopped suddenly, shoving the transformer into his coat pocket. "Maureen!" he exclaimed in his heartiest, friendliest voice. "I didn't see you back there. But I'm glad you came in. I've got some more leaflets for you to hand out to the other classes."

Maureen was so terrified that she couldn't move. For a moment she thought she was actually going crazy with fear, because it seemed that a monkey's face was peering out of the jungle of plants around the divider. Then the monkey put its forefinger to its lips—and she realized that Marvin must have sneaked into the office before Mr. Costue came back.

"Here you go, Maureen." Mr. Costue strode around the divider, holding out the leaflets and beaming. But to Mr. Fader he spoke aside in a low, sharp voice: "I told you not to let anyone in while I was gone."

Mr. Fader hung his head. "I didn't mean to, Will. She . . . just came in. I thought you had locked the door. Don't worry, though. I explained pretty well. She was quite impressed with the flag, too."

"The flag!" Mr. Costue reared back and stared at his partner, his pink face turning red. "You showed her the flag? You idiot! I should lock you in a closet with the computer and make you—" Whirling toward Maureen, he seized her arm. "What did he tell you?"

Maureen shrank back, but Mr. Costue's big pink hand held her fast. "N-nothing," she stammered, trying to look stupid.

"I'm sorry, Will." Mr. Fader cringed, gazing at Mr. Costue with pleading eyes. "I tried to explain your wonderful plan for the country, and she seemed to understand, but then she said you weren't my friend. We're the best of friends, aren't we, Will?"

Mr. Costue's face seemed to swell like a red balloon, and Maureen wondered if he was going to explode. Then he let out his breath and smiled, making his eyes twinkle. "Of course we are, Horace. You and me, old buddy, forever and ever—Costue and Fader, the winning team!" He glanced at Maureen, his pale eyes piercing her like a laser. "But we've got a problem here, old buddy, because now this girl knows about the Plan. And we can't have that, old buddy."

"But you can explain it to her, Will," said Mr. Fader. "I probably didn't explain it very well, after all."

"I—I like your plan a lot." Maureen's teeth were chattering so that she could hardly speak. "I think it's great."

Mr. Costue laughed gently, shaking his head. "Horace doesn't understand people very well. He's just a molecular biologist. But I understand you, Maureen. So we're going to have to take care of you, Maureen." Pulling her toward him, Mr. Costue reached out to the top of Maureen's head. She felt a twinge in her scalp. "Here, Horace. Feed this hair into the DNA decoding unit. Then we'll turn her back to—oh, say, one or two years old. Too young to tell anyone the Plan."

Gazing at Mr. Costue with his doglike eyes, Mr. Fader took the hair. "Right, Will."

"Mr. Fader," Maureen tried to say, but nothing came out. "Mr. Fader!" she croaked. "You can't trust him. Check the data bank. Just check it, that's all."

Mr. Costue's grip on her arm tightened. "What is she talking about, Horace?"

Mr. Fader looked at the floor, fiddling with the hair. "My name in the data bank. But I didn't believe her for a second, Will. I always trusted you. It's going to be you and me, running the world, right, Will?"

"That's right, Horace." Mr. Costue's voice was like syrup. "Feed her hair into the decoding unit, Horace. I'll plug in a transformer." Taking the transformer from his jacket pocket, he stepped toward the wall outlet, dragging Maureen with him.

"Check the data bank, Mr. Fader!" she screamed.

"Hurry up," barked Mr. Costue over his shoulder. "She could ruin our Plan, Horace." He jammed the transformer into the outlet.

Maureen began to sob. In a few minutes she would be a babbling toddler. Why didn't Marvin go get the police? "Marvin, help!"

Mr. Costue gave her arm a twist. "Who's Marvin?"

But Mr. Fader was clearing his throat. "Er . . . It wouldn't hurt your feelings if I checked the data bank for my name first, would it, Will?"

Mr. Costue and Maureen both stared at him. Maureen's heart fluttered. "If he's really your friend, he won't mind, Mr. Fader."

"You're pushing me, Horace," warned Mr. Costue. "I'm your only friend in the world. Who else would even hire you, you with your crackpot ideas about cloning people from lemon gelatin? Ha-ha!"

Maureen saw Mr. Fader flinch and stiffen. "If he's your friend, Mr. Fader, why is he talking about you like that? Check—" Mr. Costue's meaty hand clamped over her mouth, smothering her words.

"Come on, Horace," he said.

But Mr. Fader hesitated, holding Maureen's hair between his thumb and forefinger. He looked from Mr. Costue to the computer terminal, and back again. "I'm just going to check, Will," he said apologetically. "It would set my mind at rest." Sitting down in front of the keyboard, he began to tap.

"Stop that!" bellowed Mr. Costue. He tried to go for Mr. Fader, but Maureen pulled the other way as hard as she could. "Touch one more key and we're through, Fader!"

But Mr. Fader was not listening. He was staring at the gray screen. As Mr. Costue staggered up behind him, dragging Maureen, she read the white letters:

HORACE BINDLE FADER
READY TO TRANSFORM

Mr. Fader's left hand opened, letting the long brown hair fall to the floor.

Releasing Maureen's arm, Mr. Costue lunged for Mr. Fader's back. Maureen leaped after him, clutching at his striped coattail.

Then there was a shriek like a battle cry. Maureen jerked her head up to see Marvin crouched on top of the divider, hefting a spider plant. "Take this, clone!"

Stopping short, Mr. Costue glanced up in time to see the potted plant coming at him. He ducked, catching the pot on his shoulder instead of his head, but it threw him off balance. Stumbling backward over Maureen, he fell heavily, hitting his head against a filing cabinet. He groaned once and then lay still.

Maureen, who had managed to roll out of his way, scrambled to her feet. "Stop, Marvin!"

Marvin hesitated, holding a second potted spider plant ready to heave at Mr. Fader. "Down with clones!" he said, not quite so loudly. "Why?"

"Because . . . *he's* okay."

Stepping through the mess of potting soil and fragments of crockery and spider plant leaves, Mr. Fader bent over Mr. Costue's striped-coated bulk. "Will, my only friend!" He picked up his wrist to feel his pulse. "You're all right, Will. . . . But how could you? Why didn't you trust me? Now I can never trust *you* again, ever." He squatted beside Mr. Costue, his lank hair hanging forward from his bowed head. "Unless . . ." Something seemed to be working in his mind, lifting his sagging features. Slowly he reached out his hand, plucked a wavy gray hair from Mr. Costue's head. Slowly he retraced his steps to the computer.

As Maureen and Marvin watched, he opened a drawer underneath the computer terminal, stretched the hair out in a narrow groove, and closed the drawer. Then he began to tap the keys.

Letters appeared on the screen:

```
WILLIAM  C.  COSTUE
DNA  DATA  PROCESSED
READY  TO  TRANSFORM
```

"Good-bye, Will." Mr. Fader's voice was choked. He tapped again, and the screen flashed:

```
AGE  3
```

He pulled a lever beside the keyboard.

Ploom!

As if slammed by an invisible hand, Marvin toppled into the palms on the other side of the divider. Mr. Fader sprawled over the computer terminal, and Maureen, staggered back against the filing cabinet. With mixed horror and hope she gazed down at Mr. Costue —and let her breath out shakily.

Mr. Costue's coat and trousers, stretched out on the floor beneath a brown cloud, were almost flat. A pair of small bare feet stuck out from the bottom of the striped coat. Brown drops fell from the cloud to drench the carpet all around the coat.

"You did it, Mr. Fader," said Maureen, gagging at the smell of burning egg white. "You saved everybody —the whole country."

"That was perfect!" Marvin bounded around the divider, rubbing his bruises. "The perfect solution! The perfect revenge!" He stared admiringly at the little feet sticking out of Mr. Costue's coat.

But Mr. Fader sat at the computer terminal with his face in his hands, his drooping shoulders shaking. He's lost his only friend in the world, thought Maureen. She moved closer to him. "Don't cry, Mr. Fader. Your friend Will is still here. He's just a different—size." She searched for something more cheering to say. "Maybe you'll be even better friends now."

Mr. Fader raised his tear-stained face. "Do you really think so?"

"Sure. . . ." Then Maureen remembered with a shock why she had come here in the first place. "Oh! Mr. Fader, please—right now—please turn my mother back: Kathleen MacQueen Harrity, age thirty-eight."

Mr. Fader let out a deep sigh. "Why not? The Plan is out of the question, now." He began to tap the keyboard.

KATHLEEN MACQUEEN HARRITY
READY TO REVERSE TRANSFORMATION
AGE 38

"Yeah!" Marvin hovered behind Mr. Fader, his face alight.

Hand on the lever, Mr. Fader hesitated. "Is your mother near the site of the original transformation?"

"What do you mean?" asked Maureen. "I think she's in the kitchen right now."

Mr. Fader looked worried. "It would be better if she was at the spot where she was first transformed. Then the organic residue"—he motioned to the brown splotches on the carpet—"could be reabsorbed." As

Maureen stared blankly, he explained, "There's several more pounds of your mother than there are of your friend, you know. It has to come from somewhere."

Maureen's heart sank as she remembered all her hard work the night before with the spray cleaner and paper towels. "The icky brown stuff in the office? I wiped it all up."

"Oh, dear." Mr. Fader frowned at the screen.

Marvin, now sitting on the cabinet beside the terminal with his legs dangling, spoke up. "What if we gave her some protein right away? It wouldn't have to be the same protein that was—uh—left over in the first place, would it?"

Mr. Fader glanced up at Marvin with surprise and respect. "No. As a matter of fact, any protein and liquid mix might do. Maybe it'll work out all right." He turned back to Maureen. "Do you have some lemon gelatin powder at home? If you can quickly stir that with a quart of water and half a teaspoon of salt, and make her drink it . . ." He pulled down the lever. "But you'd better hurry."

Letters blinked on the screen:

KATHLEEN MACQUEEN HARRITY
TRANSFORMATION REVERSED

Maureen hadn't thought about where the rest of her mother was going to come from. What if her mother turned out all scrawny, just because Maureen had

wiped up the brown splotches? And now she had to
pedal all the way back home, part of it uphill, with her
foot throbbing more than ever.

"Come *on*!" Marvin was halfway to the door, beck-
oning urgently. "No time to waste—the victim of the
clone plot needs protein."

Surprised but grateful, Maureen limped after him.
She had to ride her bike all the way back home, but not
by herself. She had to face what had happened to her
mother—but Marvin was coming with her to help.

As Maureen reached the door they heard a little
voice whimpering, and paused to listen. Mr. Fader's
voice crooned, "It's all right, Willy. You just bumped
your head."

"Willy bump," sobbed the little voice.

"It was a bad bump, but Willy's a brave boy."
Through the palm fronds they saw Mr. Fader standing
up, the striped coat gathered into his arms. "Uncle
Horace make it all better. Uncle Horace take care of
Willy." He rocked the bundle. "First we go buy Willy
nice new clothes. Then we get ice cream for Willy."

"Ice cweam?" whined the voice. "Willy want beer!"

Maureen found herself giggling, and Marvin
grinned. "The Revenge of the Alien Clones," he said,
as if it were a comic book title. His eyes sparkled.
"Well, come on! I'll follow you."

12

Back to Best Friends?

All the way home, Maureen was thankfully aware of Marvin pedaling just behind her. Now and then she glanced back at his eager Curious George face, bent over his handlebars. Pain stabbed through her left foot every time she pressed down on it, but she could stand it. She could stand it down Main Street as far as Cooper Street, up Cooper to Chestnut Hill Road. . . .

And finally Maureen was dropping her bicycle on the driveway, staggering up the garden steps with Marvin at her heels. They burst into the kitchen to find Alison standing in the middle of the room, howling. Maureen's mother lay sprawled on her back near the sink, her eyes closed. "The clone victim," breathed Marvin. The jeans Mrs. Harrity was wearing had popped open at the waist, and her red striped polo shirt

139

pulled tightly under her arms. Was she all right?

"Alison, stop that bawling!" Maureen dropped to the floor beside her mother. Mrs. Harrity moaned and opened her mouth a little, but only a croak came out.

"The protein solution! Where's the lemon gelatin?" Clambering onto the counter, Marvin rummaged through the cupboard. "Here it is. Quart jar?" But Maureen had already pulled an empty mayonnaise jar from another cupboard. While Marvin mixed the gelatin with water from the sink, Maureen got out the salt and spooned half a teaspoon into the jar.

"Alison, hold up Mom's head." Kneeling, Maureen put the jar to her mother's lips.

With her eyes still closed, Mrs. Harrity swallowed a sip. She grimaced, but then she gulped down half of the liquid in the jar without stopping.

"Mommy!" whimpered Alison. "Are you okay, Mommy?"

Maureen felt like whimpering, too. "Mom?"

Mrs. Harrity's eyes opened. She focused on Maureen bending over her, then put her head back to look at Alison and Marvin. Her eyes widened. "What is going on here?" She pushed herself up on one elbow. "What in the—never mind." Her voice cracked. "Give me that jar." She sat up, drained the rest of the salty lemon gelatin mixture, and shuddered. "Why am I so cold, in the month of June? I'm *freezing*."

"Mrs. Harrity," said Marvin solemnly, "I'm afraid you've been the victim of a clone plot."

"The turkey," whispered Maureen. A source of protein! She had forgotten about the frozen turkey. Mom must have absorbed it in the moment of transformation.

Alison jumped up. "Mommy, I didn't mean to hurt Maureen's foot. It wasn't my fault. The turkey just fell, by accident."

"Alison," said Maureen urgently. "Go get Mom's bathrobe. She's cold." She had to get her mother out of the clothes Kitty had borrowed before Mom had a chance to start wondering about them.

"What turkey?" Bewildered, Mrs. Harrity looked from Alison to Marvin. "And who's this, Maureen— a friend of yours from school?"

Maureen nudged Alison's leg. "Go get the bathrobe!" As Alison trotted off down the hall, Maureen untied her mother's sneakers. "Yeah, this is Marvin Smith. Er— We were going to have turkey for dinner, Mom. I was going to cook it for you, since you fainted." Maureen babbled as she worked the sneakers Kitty had borrowed off of her mother's feet and helped her squirm out of Maureen's jeans. "Oh, Mom, I'm so glad you're . . . feeling better."

"Well," said Marvin in a loud voice, "I guess I'd better be going." Turning his red face away, he was edging toward the door—embarrassed that her mother was changing her clothes, Maureen realized. His last words came out in a rapid chatter. "Nice to meet you, Mrs. Harrity. Thanks for having me over, Maureen. See you tomorrow." The door closed behind him.

Mrs. Harrity sat up and pulled on the bathrobe that Alison was holding out. "You kids are a bunch of turkeys, yourselves. Did Alison really drop something on your foot, Maureen?" Slowly she pushed herself up from the floor. "Ooh. I'm still dizzy."

Hoping to change the subject before the whereabouts of the frozen turkey came up again, Maureen was relieved to hear the telephone ring. "I'll get it."

"If it's for me," said her mother, tying the sash of her bathrobe, "tell them I'm taking a nap, and I'll—Maureen, you're limping."

But it was Tracey.

"Hi, Maureen." Tracey laughed a little, as if to say that Maureen might think there was something wrong between them, but that was a silly thought. "Hi."

"Well, hi," said Maureen.

"I was just thinking about the field trip tomorrow." Clearing her throat, Tracey went on in a carefully casual voice. "Is Kitty still there?"

"Kitty?" Maureen looked at her mother, now sitting at the kitchen table and gulping down a glass of milk. "No, not . . . No, she isn't."

"You mean she went back to New Hampshire?" There was a happy note in Tracey's voice. "Then she can't come on the field trip."

"No." Maureen sighed heavily. After all she had been through! Almost losing her mother, almost getting turned into a two-year-old, hurting her foot—to say nothing of all her hard work and planning, and her

143

embarrassment at school this morning. And still she didn't have a partner for the field trip.

"That's too bad," said Tracey. "I was just thinking . . . I'm not so sure I want to be partners with Gwen on the field trip. She's kind of a snob about being a good swimmer, and sometimes she isn't very nice."

"Did you tell her you didn't want to be her partner?" asked Maureen.

"No, not yet. I thought I'd talk to you first, and see if you wanted to be partners with me." When Maureen didn't answer right away, Tracey went on, "I'm—I'm really sorry if I hurt your feelings."

With a funny feeling, Maureen realized that this was exactly what she had longed for, only two days ago. It seemed like two months ago. Then Maureen had thought the only thing that could make her happy was Tracey changing her mind and apologizing and offering to be Maureen's partner on the field trip, after all. But now Maureen didn't feel especially overjoyed. She opened her mouth to say, "Well, all right." Then she shut it again.

"Are you still mad at me?" asked Tracey.

"No. . . ." Maureen was surprised to realize that she actually wasn't mad at Tracey anymore. But she wasn't thrilled at the prospect of being her partner, either.

Two days ago, Maureen had wanted more than anything to go back to being Tracey's best friend, back to that snug, warm, down-vest feeling. But now the idea was about as appealing as a plate of school cafeteria spaghetti.

She couldn't go backwards now! Not after saving Mom and Dad and Jody and Alison from Mr. Costue and his United Friends. Not after she and Marvin had triumphantly defeated the alien clone plot.

Thinking about Marvin and Jody, Maureen found herself smiling. And then it dawned on her that she didn't *need* to go backwards. "Thanks for asking me, Tracey, but Jody already asked if I wanted to be partners on the field trip with her and Amanda. Anyway, don't you think it would hurt Gwen's—"

"Maureen!" Her mother's voice interrupted. "What are you talking about, going on the field trip with a hurt foot? You are not going anywhere except to the hospital, to get that X-rayed."

"Oh." Maureen looked down at her foot, which certainly was still throbbing. "Oh, right. Tracey, I can't go anyway, because I can't go hiking—I hurt my foot."

"Oh, really? How did that happen?"

How did that happen! Maureen shook her head. "I can't explain now." She didn't think she would ever tell Tracey what had happened. She might tell Jody, though, so that Jody wouldn't go on believing in friend insurance. And she might tell Marvin, who already knew most of it, anyway.

She saw her mother making motions for her to get

145

off the phone. "Anyway, I have to go. 'Bye, Tracey."

Hanging up the phone, Maureen noticed that her mother seemed thin-faced and pale. "Are you all right, Mom?"

Her mother smoothed back her hair, smiling at Maureen. "Yes, darling. I'm sorry I scared you and Alison." Standing up, she put an arm around each girl and hugged them. Maureen, nuzzling against her mother's shoulder, sighed a sigh of pleasure. Her head fit just under Mom's chin, which was the way it should be.

"I guess I've been studying too hard," Mrs. Harrity went on. "Fainting like that! I'd better rest before I drive you to the hospital. And meanwhile"—she looked sternly down at Maureen—"I want *you* to lie on the sofa with that foot up. You can read a book or something, but no more running around, do you understand?"

"Okay." Maureen felt a wave of relief washing over her. Maureen didn't have to be in charge anymore! Her mother was back, telling her what to do. Mom was a fine mother—a much better mother than she was a friend.

"I'll keep Maureen company." Alison's voice was almost as stern as her mother's. "She can tell me a story."

Hobbling into the family room and sinking down into the sofa, Maureen felt all her tendons go loose, as if she were suddenly unstrung. In the distance, it seemed, her left foot pulsed.

Maureen knew that she was going to have to do some fancy explaining to Alison. And later, when Mom started putting one odd thing and another together, Maureen would have to explain to *her* things like what happened to the turkey that fell on Maureen's foot.

But right now, Maureen could just lie back and gaze through the window behind the sofa at the fading light flickering in the maple leaves. She felt lucky to have Mom and Dad and even Alison, lucky to know kids like Jody and Marvin. Lucky that she didn't need friend insurance.

JUL 1 6 1984
★JUL 1 8 1984

3 1027 00148 6966
THE HEWLETT-WOODMERE PUBLIC LIBRARY

WITHDRAWN

J FIC Gormley
Gormley, Beatrice.
Best friend insurance

BOOK
SALE

28 MAY NOT BE
DAY
BOOK RENEWED

Hewlett-Woodmere Public Library
Hewlett, New York 11557

Business Phone 516-374-1967
Recorded Announcements 516-374-1667

260